Dark Rise: The Nightmares' Isolation

John W. Rahway

2

Chapter One

Departing Ultimatum

Seventeen-year-old Raven lay trying to sleep in a rusty camp bed; its tattered sheets and filthy duvet up to her jaw. Nightmares flashed through her mind, forcing her to relive her fears of when she was undergoing the endurance tests. Unconscious tears of distress were flowing down her face, as they spilled onto the corners of her mouth. She felt alone and helplessly manipulated. This endurance test had comprised of being sent down into the freezing cold basement, being forced to stay calm while the red and silver brindle Japanese Akita dog had bit her arm. Her eyelids fluttered open as she relived the fear. The curtains were open; she could see the pitch-black sky, its moon, an aerially suspended lamp, so serene, a beacon of hope.

Raven slowly rose, wincing from pain in her bandaged, wounded arm, she gently rubbed her eyes, before glancing at the clock on the wall; it was ten past two in the morning. Raven was up, while it seemed, everyone else in this dilapidated hostel was sound asleep.

She staggered towards the bathroom. It was filthy. Despite her disgust, she showered in freezing cold water.

Alert and invigorated, "Why am I here?" She sat back down on the bed, in a state of deep thought, her eyes fixed on the floor as she tried to recollect. She couldn't recall a single thing from her past other than the dog biting her.

Searching the cupboard for something warm to wear, her eyes widened upon finding a menacing looking dagger wrapped up in a long cloak, she gratefully wrapped the cloak round her, feeling suddenly very mysterious and strong! It was freezing cold outside, but she was determined to leave. She tried to make sense of her situation, but all she could remember was the Akita biting her and her name. This haunted her. She adjusted the hood to hide her face, picked up the dagger and slunk out of the room.

Heart thumping, she moved noiselessly down the stairs, anxiously listening for any sounds. If caught, she feared she would be locked in the basement with that bloodthirsty dog.

It distressed her to realize that she had amnesia, but now there was nothing she could do except hope that some sight or sound would trigger her memory. She moved down the hall, listening and observing for anything unusual.

Suddenly, Raven's ears pricked up, she heard voices in the kitchen below, one voice pleading, tearful and repentant, while the other hard, angry, and cruel. Someone was in trouble! A slapping sound followed by a sob and then a cry. She continued her quiet descent, tiptoeing to the sound of sobs.

"You're going to the basement, you disgusting little thief." The angry voice said.

"B-b-b-but, Lady Smith, I'm really sorry, I just wanted a snack." The repentant voice replied.

"Just wanted a snack, you disgusting cretin! You're up six hours past curfew, you're going to the basement, so don't even try buttering me up!"

"I'm really; really sorry, just please don't send me to that horrible dog."

"You stupid girl, you should have thought about that before stealing food."

Raven's eyes darted towards the hallway below, and saw a young girl with pale skin, silver blonde hair, and the most frightened ice blue eyes, running out of the kitchen; tears streaming down her face. Raven recognized Lady Smith the cruel hostel owner maliciously following her, swinging her cane, to strike the girl's legs as she ran. Raven hated seeing anyone hurt or abused.

Desperate to help, Raven saw an old-fashioned CCTV camera above her that Lady Smith used to film the young people, to keep them under control. Quick as a flash, she decided to turn the tables on Lady Smith and take it as evidence to put Lady Smith away. She dashed, grabbing a large tape from the dilapidated CCTV camera, stuffing it in her trousers, heart thumping, rushed towards the door, which was locked.

The backs of her legs swelling angrily, the blonde-haired girl ran up the stairs desperately passing Raven a pleading look. This fired up Raven to stand up to the bully.

Anger and hatred surging through her veins, Raven prepared to confront Lady Smith.

Lady Smith was striding towards her.

"No way." Raven breathed.

The pain in her arm was excruciating, she could see Lady Smith taking sick pleasure at her discomfort. Smith reached Raven, seizing her arm.

"Going somewhere, missy." she said coolly.

Raven struggled as Lady Smith pulled. Kicking out hard, she knocked the woman back several steps. Smith recovered, and advanced on the amnesiac, Raven kicked out again. Suddenly, a whispering voice assaulted Raven's ears.

"Kill her, she mistreated others." The voice hissed.

"Who said that?" asked Raven.

"Your friend and guardian" asserted the whisperer.

"No, I won't do it." Said Raven visibly shocked.

"You know you want to." insisted the voice.

"I'm not going to." Raven said quickly.

Raven's anger could have easily killed Lady Smith, egged on by the voices in her head.

Retrieving the dagger from her cloak and pointing it at Smith, Raven regained composure.

"If you ever treat anyone like that again, you'll be locked up." Raven threatened.

"Are you threatening me?" snarled Lady Smith.

"I have the tape, and I'll show it to the police." snapped Raven. "NOW, BACK OFF!"

Taken aback, Lady Smith hesitated. Without a moment to waste, Raven swung herself out of the window, using her hand to stabilize herself as she hit the concrete ground outside.

Meanwhile........... at Raven's school,

"Raven's still missing, the police haven't found anything. Mum's out of her mind imagining the worst, even the dog is distressed!" Raven's older sister Amber confided.

"Even if there's foul play, she's more than a match for anyone and she'll be back, she's a clever girl." Sajid comforted.

"Hopefully not 'til after I bag the head girl position." Victoria kept her thoughts to herself but said "Don't worry I'm sure she'll be back soon."

Dark Rise: The Nightmares' Isolation

Chapter Two

The Night Journey

*W*rapping her cloak round for warmth, she rushed away. Frightened by the thought of who could be following her and frightened by what lay ahead. She hurried to put distance between herself and the hostel. Not aware, who inhabited streets, at this time of night, her anxious thoughts hammered at her brain as she turned into the shadows.

The pain in Raven's arm was searing, she held it as she walked. She scanned the streets and prayed for safety. She was penniless; perhaps she could use her jewellery to pay her way. As far as she could see nobody was following her, but she could see red and blue lights flashing in the distance.

The red and blue colors were good to see. The police were out, their destination unknown.

Exhausted and hurting she sat on a dark footpath off the main road, her back resting on a low brick wall, strangely comforted by the presence of the police going about their business.

Half an hour later, Raven stood back up, the rest had helped, and she was able to think properly. She resumed her journey, but not before giving the officers the tape from the hostel, the officer looked at her curiously, but had more important things on his mind. Raven didn't miss the quizzical look in his eyes and wondered if he recognized her-or if she had imagined it. Perhaps she should have asked for help. Observing the dark streets and cold steel shop shutters, she realized she was wandering aimlessly. Not knowing and being alone made her feel vulnerable.

Raven thought again about her lost memories, her past, her family and friends. She wished she knew who she was, where she belonged but where would she begin her search.

Walking on, she came across a sign to a tourist attraction, a castle that showcased weapons from the past, present and future in its grounds. There was a sign with directions. She decided to follow the sign.

"Fantastic, I'll feel less vulnerable with another weapon!" Raven smiled.

This should have been an easy walk, especially because she was young. But she was feeling weak and famished. She was not sure when she'd last eaten; but it probably hadn't been for a while.

"Without food, I don't know if I'll be able to find my past or the castle." grumbled Raven.

Though nobody seemed to be around, Raven remained ever vigilant, dragging herself on, and keeping an eye open for something to eat. She saw a twenty-four café that truckers used, just ahead, a ray of hope plucked at her.

She rushed towards the cafe, hopeful that there would be food in there. Through the window, she could see some truck drivers eating and instinct told her not to go in, because questions would be raised as to why she was all alone, and she could be vulnerable.

This was unfamiliar territory, and she could end up hurt or killed. There was a woman in the yard throwing the day's leftovers, so she swiped a box containing cooked meat, bread and kebab before sneaking away. But to her dismay, her path was blocked by a huge black and tan Doberman pinscher.

The Doberman stood still; eyes blazing while his mouth frothed. With a snarl, he charged forwards. She stood still, as the great beast headed towards her.

Raven composed herself and moved aside. The Doberman flung himself into thin air, but turning around, he prepared to fly at her. Quickly, she took some meat from the box and flung it towards him, calming and busying him whilst satiating his hunger.

While the Doberman ate, she snuck away to eat ravenously, satisfying her own hunger. Energized, she headed away towards the castle. The rest of the walk wasn't at all bad, although the cold numbed her fingers.

Raven reached into her cloak, and found a flask of water. She opened it carefully, and took a sip.

Much to her surprise the pain in her arm disappeared immediately and she felt strengthened.

"What's going on?" breathed Raven. "I feel so much better"

She realized it was the water; it healed and emboldened her. However, this meant she would have to use it sparingly. Feeling full of strength, her confidence returned. She was thrilled by this find. It gave her courage. If she got hurt, she could heal. This made her feel brave and ready to take on anything.

Before long, she was in the tourist attraction; the castle and its grounds were spacious and heavily equipped with old fashioned cannons looking out over the cliff towards the sea, and a few modern day tanks on display and a section with futuristic weapons which used lightning, laser and radio frequency. At first, it appeared that nobody was there, but she was mistaken, for a blacksmith was standing by the iron forge. Raven lowered the hood of her cloak; her hair gracefully tumbled to her waist, contrasting with her skin. She looked around inquisitively.

"Excuse me, sir?" asked Raven.

The blacksmith ignored her, she called again, and he still ignored her. He seemed to be some hologram. Raven picked up a war scythe with a silver handle and a sharp upward pointing purple blade, extending from the open beak of a raven (her namesake).

"I'm offering my watch in return for this weapon, would you accept this as payment for the scythe?" still no response. So, she put her watch back on her wrist and slowly, purposefully made to walk out to see if anyone would stop her! No one did. She turned around again to allow time for someone to come and receive payment, still nobody came, so she decided to slowly walk away with the scythe in hand. Still unsure how to pay, she retraced her footsteps and left. Raven walked away from the castle, in a good mood, having acquired a weapon. She was also pleased she didn't have to part with her watch because having lost all her memories in her past, she could log her new memories and they wouldn't be just inside her mind but also on an external gadget, a backup! She had already started to log her new journey and thoughts into her watch, she would just often investigate the memory function, and it would hear her thoughts and create new memories both from verbal outpourings and silent thoughts. She would just have to find another way to pay for the scythe because her watch was too important to part with.

Although exhausted, Raven continued walking. Walking made her feel safer, calmer, and helped her make sense of her thoughts. But then, a sharp pain shot through her head, and she heard a soft whispering voice.

"Go to the forest, you'll find the answer there." the voice said gruffly.

"Who's there?" snarled Raven.

Raven clasped her head, trying to suppress the voice. She recognized the voice; it was the same voice that had told her to kill Lady Smith. Why was she hearing these voices? Who was trying to control her thoughts and actions?

She felt unsettled and confused.

Raven continued to walk through the great many streets, often losing her way. She couldn't see a single person, save for the odd car driving past but she could hear crows cawing announcing the approaching dawn.

She saw the sign for the forest and having no other clues she followed the arrow.

Having identified the location of the forest, she decided to take a rest. However, the footpath was less than comfortable.

She made her way towards a house with a skip full of items and found some blankets and lifted them out gratefully.

Entering through the house's side gate into a concealed area of the back-garden Raven found an unlocked shed, a place to rest. She had never been so tired, all that walking, especially without food or drink had practically finished her off. Shutting her cat-like blue eyes, a tidal wave of sadness brimmed over, but mercifully sleep overcame sadness, healing peaceful sleep. Rested, she opened her eyes groggily and wondered how long she had slept. The sleep had helped, but immediately she remembered the rasping voice instructing her to go to the forest. Had she just imagined it? Curiosity got the better of her, and she decided that she would go to the forest.

    It was daylight and without cover of darkness she had to sneak out of the property.

Dark Rise: The Nightmares' Isolation

Chapter Three

Deal with the Devil

A dense canopy of tall trees was in sight. Raven couldn't help feeling vulnerable and thought.

"What good will come of me going into the forest, will I find any of my memories here?" Raven thought anxiously. *"Or am I just listening to the whispers of my mind?"*

She stood still, thinking frantically, her loneliness, chilling, but at least in sunlight, the forest looked beautiful.

The mystery of the forest sent a chill down her spine, as she engaged in a mental debate with herself, as to how it could possibly lead her back to her past.

Feeling a shroud of dark energy flowing towards her, she stood still, transfixed, to tune in to an invisible approach, her heart almost stopping. A mist spun in a vortex, dancing like a whirlpool.

Realizing she wasn't alone; she felt a strange and sinister presence nearby.

"Raven, I have the key to all of your memories, but in return I need all six of the precious gems." the voice explained.

"Who are you, how do you know I'm Raven and what are you talking about? Why should I get you the precious gems?" Raven shot back.

"If you bring me all six precious gems which are in the five realms of fear, I will restore all of your memories. In spite of herself, Raven listened. "Of the six gems, the first is the emerald which is in The Nightmare Rift. You shall find out where the others are after you find the emerald. You will not be alone because an angel knight will guide and accompany you; he knows how to cross over to each realm, he can transcend time under certain conditions. Use this ring, its glow brightens when you get near the gems." A silver ring floated from the mist towards Raven.

"Why do you want them and why me?" asked Raven.

"You have some very special abilities, Raven, that no one else possesses and I have mastery over the Seven Deadly Sins, and in case you are wondering, they are: Wrath, Lust, Envy, Sloth, Gluttony, Greed and Pride." Boomed the gloating voice "With these gems I can make people kill one another, when people cannot control their envy, greed and anger, they take to crime and cause wars between themselves. Man never learns from history or his past mistakes when millions die in war and destruction. But think of how powerful I could be if I could also control kindness, compassion, love, diligence, trust and humility too, because as you see people with these qualities come to the aid of those left over from the destruction.

"You will help me get that power or you will never have your memories back and you will not know where you belong or who your family and friends are." The voice warned.

"How is it possible someone like you will honour your word?" responded Raven. "Reveal yourself! Come out of the mist!"

"Once you find the gems and hand me the gems, I shall give you your memories back, as your memories will be no good to me." The voice continued.

Unable to trust him but with no alternative, Raven skeptically decided to explore this option.

She felt as though she was being watched and manipulated.

"If he knows the truth about my past whether I like it or not, I'm going to have to believe him and the only way to do that is to comply for now." thought Raven. *"But I can't possibly hand over the precious gems to him. I can't possibly help him increase his power so much that he will destroy all humanity by setting them up against each other and fighting one another for land, for money till the complete*

end. But I'll have to fall in with his game 'til I have the gems. Once he takes the gems from me, he will dispose of me too as he won't need me anymore. Basically, I need to find them and preserve them in safety away from him. The world needs compassion, kindness, love and diligence to heal, help and create harmony and health. No, sir! I'll find the precious gems-but definitely not for you to get your hands on them. I am going to play along with you 'til I find them."

Thinking it through, she reached forwards and took the ring from the mist and put it on her index finger. Taking this to be her acceptance of the deal he melted away.

Shocked and confused, she wondered if she had imagined this dialogue.

Unsure of what to do next she decided to move away from this spot and give herself time to think. She looked at her hands and there it was; the ring!

Amber's sleep was disturbed by dreams of Raven, forests and unknown whisperers. Did these dreams carry a message? Awake, she reflected, her younger sister was respected, popular for her sporting prowess and helpful nature.

"No, she had no reason to run away!"

Dark Rise: The Nightmares' Isolation

Chapter Four

An Act Of Compassion

Slithering through the forest, Raven barely noticed the trees and wildflowers. Perplexed about her lost past, fearing for her future, she had a lot to think about. She wanted to find her memories, but had no intention to obey the whisperer with his twisted plans. She would play along, whilst she thought of a solution to her dilemma. She was alone and vulnerable but not stupid! There was surely a way to connect to her family that didn't rely on the veiled whisperer. She knew his word meant nothing, but still she wondered when the angel knight he had mentioned might appear to show her the way, as she had no idea where to go.

A loud, pained roar flooded the forest. The sound shocked her from her thoughts, she stood still, silent.

The roar sounded again. Unsure as to whether she was in danger or if someone else was, in this shadowy forest, Raven hid, feeling concealed eyes upon her.

Treading lightly on the muddy ground, her unease and curiosity propelled her towards the sound, struggling to keep her emotional balance.

A large barn owl screeched across her path as though to warn others of her presence, its piercing black eyes glaring.

Raven saw a fire light amidst the trees, from where the roar sounded. The light felt like a glimmer of hope but looks could be deceiving.

It was difficult to see in the descending mist; not knowing what might be hiding in the dense thicket heightened her senses.

A rustling sound came from the leaves, her eyes darted.

"What was that?" Luckily, it was just a badger, working its way to its set.

"What does this whisperer want with me, but also how does he know me, he may not know anything about me, it might be his way of manipulating me for his gems?" she thought, feeling vulnerable.

The roar ripped the air, pained and raw, followed by a loud laugh and barking. A whimper sounded soon after the laugh, then angry snarls.

She could see a roaring fire, surrounded by men, their mastiffs and a wounded grizzly bear tied to a tree. In front of the bear were two wounded dogs, unable to move.

"Bear baiting! Animal cruelty"

Horrified, she hurried carefully round the men and mastiffs, hiding herself in the shadows of trees and bushes so they wouldn't notice. When the men went up, readying their dogs for another attack on the bear, she swiftly slipped behind the bear, to cut the knot that bound its neck to the tree.

Slicing the knot with the dagger she'd taken from the hostel, she stepped back in the shadows.

"Go on, you're free now." she whispered to the bear.

The bear stayed put, glancing at Raven with its piercing brown eyes. She splashed some of her rejuvenating water on it, instantly healing its wounds. She desperately willed it with her mind to go.

"What do you think you're doing!" one of the men shouted angrily.

Oh no, she had been seen!

In a flash, she ran, in case the men set their mastiffs on her. Sure enough, one of them did but Raven turned and unsheathed her scythe. She pointed her scythe at the men, and a stream of purple lightning shot from the blade, knocking off some branches from a tree, and as the branches fell, the bear bolted, into the forest.

"You've ruined our bear baiting!" shouted another man,

The men allowed her to get away; too drunk to think she was worth the bother.

"It's just a kid."

The bear ran for its life, the cruel men stumbled after it; Raven poured a few drops of her water on the two injured dogs, healing and petting them as they followed her before dashing back to their owners. She looked at her water flask to see if any water was left. To her intense pleasure she could see it replenishing itself. She watched mesmerized.

Her thoughts then returned to her own desire of finding friends and family; she wanted the safety and warmth of a home. She also knew it was madness to trust the whisperer, but for now what choice did she have?

Amber often went into Raven's bedroom, hoping anxiously that she had perhaps come home in the middle of the night. She wondered why her sister had left without saying goodbye. Why had she just disappeared?

"It's not like Raven to go away like this; she never normally leaves without telling anyone."

Amber scoured her sister's room for any clues.

Dark Rise: The Nightmares' Isolation

Chapter Five

The Angel Knight

She couldn't shake the feeling of being watched, looking around there was no one. Still this uneasy feeling came back. Secret eyes spying, eerie and unseen!

"*How cowardly!*" she thought to comfort herself.

Seeing a small mountain range ahead, sharp, jagged rocks and tufts of green with a beautiful golden light shining upon its summit, she was strongly pulled towards it.

"I must reach that light and I'll be able to see all around for miles if I can get to the top. Then I can work out which route to follow."

As she walked her ears registered the howls of wolves, calling to one another. At least the wolves were an open enemy; still, as she struggled to shake off this feeling that someone invisible was secretively monitoring her every step. The wolves were nowhere to be seen, but she was aware, one foot in their territory could mean her end. The howls grew louder and fiercer. Whilst she liked animals, tame or wild, having a natural affinity and fascination for them, she knew it was better to be safe and not blame the animals for what is inherently their nature; hunting, chasing to eat.

"*It's ok, they're not anywhere near me.*"

Raven could make out blurred shapes. The mist made it impossible to work out what they were. Raven's eyes were watering, but these weren't tears.

"This mist and fog are preventing me seeing."

The outline became clear. Wolves!

As if reading her thoughts, hungry wolves had rushed to the mountain too, pacing, drooling, snarling in front of her, eyeing her like a plump chicken, preparing to kill. Her hair stood on end, unsheathing her scythe stealthily, deadly still, she observed the wolves' movements, assessing whether she would need to fight.

It wasn't long before the wolves advanced on Raven; she realized that she had no choice but to defend herself. This saddened her, as she had always loved and admired wolves, and she didn't want to hurt them. She backed away, the wolves advancing on her; she moved quickly, her pursuers were faster! A mighty leaping grayness knocked her to the floor.

Raven, grounded, looked up into the ice-cold eyes of a male omega wolf, standing above her, snarling, poised to attack, teeth just inches from her face. Somehow, she scrambled to her feet, grabbing her scythe, Raven faced the pack.

The omega wolf leaped again, eyes aflame, teeth bared. Raven swung her scythe, wounding him deeply midair. Howling in pain, the wolf whined and licked his wound, Raven pointed her scythe, purple lightning shooting from the blade, putting the wolf out of his misery.

The remaining wolves ganged up, amber eyes glinting with vengeance. Terrified, transfixed, Raven aimed her scythe at them, longing to run away. Wolves were now surrounding her from all sides, boxing her in, preventing her attempting escape. Cornered, frightened and helpless, faced with certain death as another grey and white wolf with a scarred face and a blind eye, leaped at her with his teeth bared, Raven raised her scythe, determined, that she would die fighting. Suddenly, a blast of white electricity struck the wolf; he hit the ground whimpering in pain, closing his eyes for the last time whispering.

"Long live the master."

The wolves ran.

Shocked but sensing someone, her eyes searched the horizon and eventually she saw him. Excited, she noticed he had a golden light above his head and folded against his back were two magnificent white feathered wings, and in a scabbard attached to his belt, was a sword. A huge light grey and white dog was standing next to him; it resembled a wolf and had a bushy tail that was carried over its back like a waving plume. An Alaskan malamute.

She looked perplexedly at the man, taking in his white wings, light, and the hilt of his sword. He seemed like the angel knight from the afterlife from the whispers.

"Who are you?" asked Raven

"I am Walker, Knight of the Eternal Gardens-Defender of Purity; I sent the lightning to save you because those wolves kill anyone who attempts to climb the mountain, you wouldn't have survived them on your own, Raven."

"How do you know my name?"

"The whisperer told me all about you." Walker told her. "He has told me to guide you through the lands of fear and we shall be going to The Nightmare Rift."

"The Nightmare Rift, that's the name that the whisperer told me!"Raven breathed."Why on earth would he want me to enter a place that sounds like a horror film?"

Raven was shocked that Walker knew her name. It was good to see another person, even though she still felt wary, she was desperate for a friend, Raven shook Walker's outstretched hand. Walker's dog approached her.

"This is Lynk"

"He's magnificent"

Raven's eyes softened and she couldn't help reaching out to stroke him, and when she did it wasn't just Lynk that felt happy. Suddenly, in her mind's eye she could see and imagine a little girl playing fetch with a friendly dog and laughing heartily. She could almost feel the grass underfoot and the fresh breeze of the sunny day in her mind. She tried to hold onto this glorious vision and work out who it was, but it faded away. Nevertheless, it left a calm and relaxed feeling within her. A feeling of connection, something or someone that was hers to reach out to. But how?

Dark Rise: The Nightmares' Isolation

John Rahway

Chapter Six

The Nightmare Rift's Opening

Following Walker's lead, it was pleasant and comforting, to journey together, and time flew. The night air was once again alive, with the distant howls of wolves and the screeches of bats. In spite of her distrust of Walker, Raven was glad of his company and conversation. Tired and hungry, forcing herself to stay awake, she tried to get to know Walker. They passed vines bearing bunches of thick dark blue concord grapes. She reached up and plucked a bunch down.

"Would you like some, Walker?"

"Yes please."

Raven handed Walker a bunch and ate hers.

Walker found a sheltered spot and they made a fire and rested and conversed. The fire and Walker's company brightened the night.

At first light Walker gently encouraged Raven to start the journey to The Nightmare Rift, a realm in which she could start her search for the gems. Having nothing to lose she set off, before long, huge prohibitive prison like walls with a humungous gate came into view, guarded by a large creature. She worked her way towards the gate, however, the outline on the top felt like a bad omen.

Ahead they looked straight at a tall iron gate with the words: "Abandon all hope of peaceful sleep all of you who enter here." inscribed on the frame above it.

The meaning of those words made Raven laugh

"Charming." She said, "Doesn't look like anybody who enters that gate will have any peace."

Suddenly her heart stopped for a split second.

It was an emerald green dragon with a head like a conker shell! A mighty dorsal sail ran from between its lime like eyes to the small of its back, peaking at over a meter in height at the crest of the thick neck throbbing with prominent arteries. Raven unsheathed her scythe. The dragon roared and a powerful blast of purple energy shot from its mouth.

Instinctively, she aimed her scythe at the dragon; the purple lightning flew from the blade and collided with the dragon's attack, causing an enormous explosion. When the smoke cleared, the dragon was unaffected and roaring furiously. The dragon flew up before shooting back down, until it was in mid-air, forcefully beating its bat like wings.

Raven braced against the burning wind from the dragon's wing beats, struggling to hold her scythe. The force was intense; she aimed her scythe at the dragon, emitting the electricity again. However, the power of the wing beats prevented it even touching the dragon.

Flying up, the dragon breathed another blast. Raven retaliated; the two blasts were explosive. The dragon shot towards her. However, she stayed still, waiting until it got close enough.

Then she slashed her scythe, wounding its shoulder. The dragon roared in agony. Furious, it struck again. However, the fire struck thin air, as Raven evaded speedily. The dragon's wound appeared healed!

"No way!"

She looked at the dragon again, a white glow shone from its crest. The dragon struck again, this time its energy hit Raven, who fell, dropping her scythe. She crawled towards her weapon, but the dragon prevented her.

"I can't give up." growled Raven.

Raven quickly drank a sip of her water, instantly reversing the damage of the dragon's attack. She waited until the dragon was above her, and seizing her scythe, she slashed its stomach.

Unfortunately, despite its wound, the dragon flew towards her, its wing knocking her down. Grounded, Raven held her scythe, and blasted the enemy. To her dismay, the dragon was unhurt.

A yellow glow shone in the dragon's eyes, as a green beam shot from its mouth. Raven saw the blast approaching, she ducked. Aiming her scythe; she projected a string of lightning once again. The dragon responded vengefully, the two blasts collided, with the dragon taking a hit.

A loud bang rang out; Raven opened her eyes and found herself down, with her scythe out of her hands. Stunned but unhurt she observed.

"The dragon keeps healing!"

She heard a voice "The dragon's neck veins supply its crest with the ability to heal itself, you can't fight the dragon and attack its neck veins at the same time, if the neck veins are untouched, it'll heal itself."

"Who's there?" Raven queried, looking behind her.

A large golden eagle sat on a tree branch, with its wings folded and eyes watching carefully.

"What do I do?"

"You distract the dragon while I attack its neck veins."

The eagle flew at the dragon's neck. Raven saw, and aimed her scythe, emitting another stream of dark violet lightning. The dragon countered; a blast shot out.

Both blasts cancelled out, as dragon became busy with the eagle. Raven aimed her scythe again; the lightning shot the dragon's chest. As the dragon was hit, she didn't realize it, but one vein was destroyed. It breathed another blast, but Raven moved quickly whilst the eagle eliminated another vein. The dragon still had the ability to heal. Raven aimed her scythe, and the lightning hit the dragon's chest.

While mid-air, the dragon beat its wings but thanks to the eagle, Raven had an opening, so she lifted her scythe, but the dragon retreated as if recognizing her abilities, her determination and mental strength.

Just as Raven was about to end it, the dragon's wing regrew, and it rose again. Raven aimed her weapon towards the dragon's head in readiness for self-defense, but she needn't have worried as the dragon conceded with a begrudging respect for the slight but fiery figure on the ground. The dragon took off in flight, circled round and alighted on top of the gate, thus signaling the end of hostilities.

Raven was confused but grateful all the same for the eagle's help.

"Why did you help me?"

"I felt sorry for you, you're so small and the dragon is so big. My name is Kindle."

Can I accompany you? I can watch and listen from above." said the eagle. "Can I ask your name?"

"I'm Raven."

The dragon spoke

"Well done, in battling me, you have proven your bravery and resourcefulness so you may now enter The Nightmare Rift."

Raven turned to Walker, fiery eyes blazing "Well we're in! No thanks to you!" Raven snarled. "You could have helped!"

Calmly, Walker spoke soothingly "Would you have learnt of your capabilities, strength and resourcefulness had I taken care of the dragon for you?, Now you know what abilities you possess and does it not make you feel more confident and less frightened? Isn't that a wonderful gift you've given yourself? Now you can travel wherever you go with self-awareness that you can look after yourself no matter the size of the enemy." His words were like cooling water to the flame of her anger.

Soothed into self-reflection she slowly stepped towards the gate.

Kindle flew ahead of Raven, who, along with Walker, entered The Nightmare Rift as the dragon blasted the door open.

During the day, outside of school times, Amber would go along with Sajid and question all the local shopkeepers and people in the neighborhood and people at bus stops where Raven was and asked when they had seen her and showed a photograph of her. She refused to believe Victoria's lies and claims that Raven had left by choice.

Dark Rise: The Nightmares' Isolation

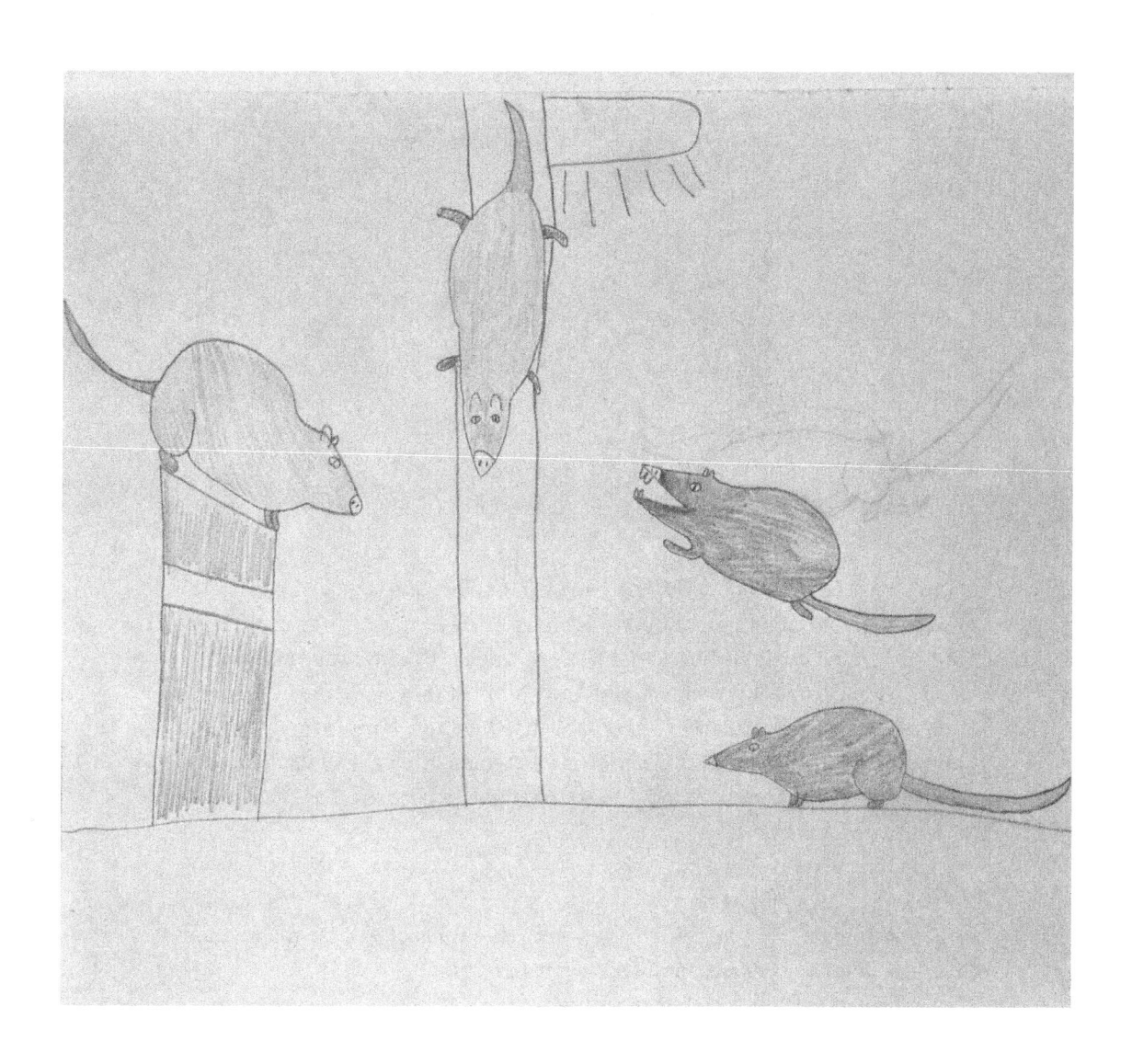

31

Chapter Seven

Pestilence Of Rats

When Raven followed Kindle, Walker and Lynk through the ominous gate, she found herself in a new realm, a different time and a horrendous scene ahead. She was unprepared for the sight of carcasses of men, women and children. Shocked and appalled to see dead bodies lying in the street, she tried to run back. The gates had slammed shut! So much death! Dreading she would die, Raven looked around the street. She saw flea-infested rats scurrying over corpses. These rats were the bearers of terrible disease and death.

"This place looks like a burial ground."

"It looks like a plague."

Raven looked over at the corpses and the amassing rats, all of them spreading disease. Her instinct was to get out. Run.

"I'd like to get out too, but we have to work through it, for the way to open."Walker asserted gently, reading her mind.

A sliver of hope washed over Raven, for she had asked Kindle to look for an exit, an escape. If anybody could find it, he could, with his bird's eye view.

"Kindle, do you see a way out?"

"I'm looking as hard as I can."

"Do you see anything, Lynk?"

"Not yet."

Raven nauseously dragged herself behind Lynk, noticing a hole in the moldy sewer cover, being gnawed at by small buck teeth.

"More rats!"

"Unfortunately, yes."

"Well let's get out of here quickly."

"Chill out, Raven."

"I'll chill out once we're out of this rat hole."

"You still haven't found a way out, have you, Kindle?" asked Raven desperately.

"I'm flying far and wide and searching as hard as I can."

"Have you found anything, Lynk?"

"No, not yet, but I'm keeping my nose to the ground."

"Well, could you both pick up the pace?"

"Stressing won't get us out."

"Fine, I'm sorry, it's just I can't stand this place."

In seconds, the hole had spread across the sewer cover, and out came a sight most horrific. A stampede of rats, some grey-brown, and others jet black with black beady eyes, charging out of the sewer.

"Let's get moving!" Raven stated irritably.

"We've got to get rid of these rats!" Walker's gentle tone reminded of the challenge.

"Let's see if there's any rat poison."

"Kindle, Lynk, can either of you find any rat poison?" Raven asked frantically.

"I thought we were looking for an exit." Kindle shot back.

"We are, but we need to get rid of these rats first to save people from disease."

"We can't leave without completing the challenge."

Seeing the disease carrying rats, Raven frantically thought of how to solve this problem. She didn't like to inflict needless pain on anything. She didn't want to be the cause of them suffering a lingering, painful and slow demise. Without any action, it meant that disease would spread and the plague would take many lives as a result. Inaction was not an option! Faced with these odds, she asked Kindle to do aerial reconnaissance and search for any cat rescues in the area and catteries. This was easy for the eagle. Having located the rescues, Kindle returned and led Raven, Walker and Lynk.

Raven was surprised to find beautiful cats of different breeds confined in small cages with just food and water. The cats had no place to exercise, nor any freedom to run and explore. Appalled, Raven saw this as injustice to the free-spirited animals that liked to climb, hunt and roam. It was a prison for cats! So, she felt justified and self-satisfied in releasing them! Sure, the owner would shout and scream and raise his fist, but there should have been better facilities than to just imprison them.

"Lynk, could you distract the owner? While Walker and I release the cats"

"Good plan, Raven."

Lynk, at Walker's command, bounded over to the owner and barked and growled at him, trapping him in his office, while Raven and Walker freed the cats, in doing so she couldn't help a chuckle. She was enjoying letting the cats go!

Raven felt this was the best course of action, to let nature take its course- the cats could again run, hunt, be free and best of all play and toy with the rats. It would hopefully reduce the chances of disease from rats and fleas, and safeguard people. The cat rescue centers should have provided the cats with a better service, more space, enrichment and play facilities.

She laughed to herself as she saw the manager red in the face, chasing the cats that were too quick for him! The felines were enjoying their freedom. He ran this way and that way, trying in vain to catch the free running cats. Raven looked to Kindle and Walker, all three of them had a quiet chuckle together, whilst Lynk chased the cats towards the rats and the cat rescue manager chased the cats. Suddenly, understanding the useful role the cats were playing, the cat rescue staff decided to encourage other cat rescues to release their cats to help. Seeing this, Raven asked him to inform all the villagers to quarantine themselves, keep distance from one another, and wear masks to prevent breathing in other germs and to clean themselves and their surroundings.

Alarmed, upon seeing an army of cats, the rats rallied and charged back, only to be eaten. Realizing their numbers were reducing, the rats made one final attempt to save themselves. Despite their efforts, the rodents soon found themselves being consumed.

With many of their numbers dead, the rats dispersed back, only for the cats to finish them.

Raven thought that the cats would return to their rightful owners having been used to human care and affection. She used her scythe to seal the sewers to prevent any more rats coming out. She, Walker and Lynk waited for Kindle to return to them, before following his lead.

"Kindle; now that the rats are gone, what do you say we get out of this cesspit?"

"I couldn't agree more, Raven."

Having found a sense of purpose and learning that she was resourceful, gave her the strength to forget her fears. Feeling braver and more confident, she stood up tall and the worried frown disappeared from her face.

A framed door with a bright light emanating appeared at the street's opposite end.

"Is this the exit?" asked Raven, feeling hopeful. "I wonder what will be next and I dread to think."

"If you look for the good, Raven, then good will appear." said Walker, as they stepped into the welcoming light.

Every day after school and an empty search, Amber would invite Sajid to come over and tick off on her lists and maps the places she had searched and where she needed to go next and make plans to expand her search. Their German shepherd dog Taz seemed to be pining for Raven; she looked at him, stroked him and said

"Perhaps you need to come on the search with me."

She started to teach him by getting him to smell Raven's clothes and hiding them round the house and asking him to go and find them, praising and rewarding him. He was a clever dog and learned it quickly. Taz's success in finding Raven's belongings added an element of fun and achievement as he returned again and again, successful, no matter how far away they hid her clothes. They laughed, giggled and celebrated and Amber said

"Taz, you're joining us on the search tomorrow."

John Rahway

Dark Rise: The Nightmares' Isolation

Chapter Eight

The Falling

Upon exiting the street, Raven breathed a sigh of relief and checked anxiously if her friends were with her. Seeing Walker, Kindle and Lynk, she laughed in a hearty way, incredulous at the cringy unpleasantness of what had just transpired, what the four of them had witnessed. They all looked at each other and laughed again, long, and loud, setting each other off again and again. The laughter was healing, cathartic and relieving of stress, distress, pain, and anxiety. Exhausted from laughing out all her fears with Kindle, Walker and Lynk-a warm, comfortable feeling engulfed her, she relaxed and found a place to sit with her friends and take in her surroundings. It was a park adjacent to a busy city centre.

"Wow, laughter really is the best medicine for both mind and body!"

Raven's stomach ached from the laughing, but it was a relieved and pleasant ache. She lay down where she was and looked at the blue sky and the white clouds moving above. Relaxed and rested, Raven felt safe with her friends, they had been a total support.

She looked around her, noticing the sprawling business center ahead, beyond the bridge that crossed the river. She could see in the distance men and women rushing about in the quest, it seemed, for money, for power, for glamour, they all wanted to be important and in control. She thought, some needed money for family needs, a home, food, heat, and clothing. Others she felt just wanted to show off; buy huge homes, cars and businesses, others wanted to buy people and be self-serving. Some however, were able to make money and share it with those less fortunate too.

"These were the most elite, though nobody realized this, they saw value in feeding and helping the poor, the homeless and oppressed. They used power and influence to benefit others too."

Raven marveled at how deceptive the world and its people are, everyone is not as they appear, it would be extremely hard to judge what really lay behind the faces people showed to the world.

She sensed she would have to get across this bridge and go to the business district to further her quest, to look for the precious gems and subsequently hope that the whisperer would honor his word and return her memories. She didn't trust him.

They made their way towards the bridge; she could see that it was called the Sifting Bridge. As she, Walker and Lynk set foot on the bridge, the bridge twisted and flung her to one side and then to the other. Walker and Lynk were unaffected, being an angel and an angel dog; they could be where they wanted. They were constrained by having to walk alongside her. As her companions, it was good to have them as friends and she was very fond of them, but again, she wondered if their loyalty was all with Mephistopheles and not with her. Kindle the golden eagle simply flew over. It looked like the test was hers and hers alone.

The bridge tipped left, to the point Raven's back collided hard with the railing on the side.

"Ugh, my back." Raven cursed

Walker took Raven's hand, helping her to an upright position. The impact of the blow was causing her to see double. Raven shook her head.

Opening her eyes, she realized that she was still on the bridge, which was now tipping to the right. Luckily, she was walking on the left side; she had grabbed the railing and steadied herself as the bridge straightened.

She deftly moved to the right side of the bridge, seizing the railing, as the bridge slipped again. Her grip reduced and she struggled to hold on.

Each time the bridge tipped; she fell to the opposite side.

Learning from this, she was able to predict the bridge's movements, Raven moved and adapted accordingly. When the bridge tipped left, she stood on the right, keeping her balance. She didn't know what force was causing the bridge to roll so violently.

Raven's heart thumped as she focused on the task at hand, moving cautiously but quickly from side to side. She realized when the bridge tipped, that she wasn't the only one falling it was every person for themselves.

Cars and buses flew about, with some landing in the river. The scene was shocking. But it was worse for those below. She realized that although some were falling, most were getting across safely. She could see some were trying to help others get to safety helping carry young children across and supporting the elderly. They seemed immune from the rocking bridge. Now she realized why it was called the Sifting Bridge, it was sorting people according to their actions. Some people were going out of their way to help others, either by repairing their broken-down cars or offering lifts, working cooperatively with people to get to safety. However, some were solely concerned for themselves and wouldn't help anyone else or work as a team. This isolated them and they became vulnerable and alone. Raven took the opportunity to reassure people that help was on the way, especially the small children terrified of the rocking and the shouts of panic.

Raven injured and tired forced herself to keep going, taking great care not to look down but trying to comfort the frightened.

"If I think of the railings as monkey bars, I could use them to negotiate the bridge." Thought Raven.

With that in mind, Raven used her hands to hold the bars, always making sure to change hands, clinging on with all her might, consistently dodging gaps; she consciously tried to save people from falling off. However, before she could even think about that, she turned her attention to the people who were below in the river to assess the situation. It was only as more cars fell into the river, that it came to her; down below she could see some emergency boats and armed service vehicles.

She had to do something to help, but she didn't know how to help or what to do. *"Perhaps if I alert them to the bridge, I could tell them to secure it and forbid anyone else from getting on."* Raven thought.

Raven did something incredibly brave, compromising her own safety she let herself down from the railing, landing precariously on an emergency services boat below.

Without hesitation, she ran to one of the officers and urged him to urgently alert all the emergency services and armed forces.

Within minutes, the armed forces and emergency services arrived, and she set about helping and asking them to secure the bridge.

The emergency services swarmed in helicopters and rescue boats to lift people from the bridge and the river.

Eventually this was done, someone from the police, fire and rescue services approached Raven.

"Thank you for your service, miss, it's much appreciated." The officer said.

Raven smiled, feeling a warm glow inside at the appreciation. In helping others, she felt as though she had also been helped in many ways. She learned about herself, her resourcefulness, and her problem-solving abilities. This raised her self-esteem and self-confidence. She felt respected and honored by those that she helped and couldn't help basking in the admiration of those looking on. Suddenly, she smiled to herself, a smile of pleasure.

Finally, the bridge was under repair.

Raven grinned with pride as she noticed Walker, Kindle and Lynk looking at her with admiration. Together, they started to leave the metropolis behind. Far in the distance, the terrain was different, steep and treacherous rocks lay ahead. So, she asked Kindle to ascertain if there was an exit, as it was time to leave this realm. Kindle effortlessly flew up and was able to advise her that that was indeed the way out. However, Raven glanced back at the district; her ears were pricked as she heard the barking of a dog. It seemed so familiar. The dog's barking pulled her heartstrings as it tugged the lead. She felt as though the dog wanted to run to her, she couldn't see the owner. She felt someone was calling her from a distance,

"Shall we go, Raven?" Walker interrupted her thoughts. "Before the way out closes?"

Raven reluctantly turned back oblivious to what she just missed.

Amber went through the family photos, she saw herself with Raven in all of them. Seeing the photos hurt Amber greatly and she wished her sister was somewhere nearby. "I really miss Raven so much, we may squabble occasionally but she's still my sister and I would give anything to have her back." Amber spoke through huge sad tears. She had decided to come home with Sajid to collect Taz to help look for Raven. They went through to the town centre and crossed the bridge to check the green and grass lands. Taz barked near the bridge and stared, Amber could see crowds of people, she scanned their faces, she tried to get him to walk on but Taz whimpered and didn't want to go. Her heartbeat quickened, she got very excited and asked Sajid to search amongst the people to help look for Raven.

The bridge had had an incident earlier it seemed, and it was impassable.

Dark Rise: The Nightmares' Isolation

Chapter Nine

Healing the Wounded

Unprepared for the sight that greeted her, Raven entered a primitive makeshift hospital, full of wounded and disfigured people. Another test! Raven was overcome with concern and to her shame, revulsion, at the horrendous injuries and pain. Fifteen people, all of whom had been gravely injured to the point they were hardly alive, lay in beds. It looked like a makeshift casualty war hospital.

"Oh my, these people are very hurt." Raven breathed.

"You can say that again, Raven." Walker replied.

"I wonder what the task is here." Kindle interjected.

"So, do I, Kindle." said Raven slowly.

Raven saw that the room was devoid of beauty. Its walls dapple grey, peeling and dirty. Tattered blue curtains, partially separated the beds from one another. All the color had gone from the curtains and the lives of the patients. The strong smell of bleach was burning her eyes.

Windows with metal jail like bars lined the far side of the room. They told a story of force and no escape.

Conflicted, she wanted to help but she also wanted to flee and get out. She walked through, catching sight of the faces of patients. Their eyes pleading for help.

Seeing the mutilated faces, terror ambushed her mind. She tried to bolt.

"I'm going to leave the way I came in!" Raven yelped. "I'm no doctor, I'm no nurse I don't think there's anything we can do for these people, I think we should try and leave the way we came in."

"Well you can't, Raven; because this is the task Mephistopheles has set for you." Walker told her.

"Mephistopheles, who's Mephistopheles," asked Raven.

"Well, Raven, the whispers you're having is Mephistopheles; he is watching you even though you can't see him. He is the one who has done the deal with you that you get your memories back providing you get the gems." Walker reminded.

Shocked, Raven turned to Walker. "Are you working for him too?"

Raven barely had time to digest this when a voice boomed from the aerial loudspeaker arrested her flight!

"You must heal all fifteen patients in fifteen minutes; the clock above you starts now!" the voice said.

She felt Walker's hand on her back calming her. "The test must be completed, Raven."

Without wanting to be, she felt propelled into action.

Looking up, she saw a clock dangling from the ceiling, with fifteen minutes flashing on it.

"How can anyone be healed in fifteen minutes?"

She looked around and on each bedside table there was medication and a syringe.

"Perhaps this is what I need to administer!" thought Raven "I'm no doctor" but she picked up the syringe.

"I'll try on the worst affected patient, what harm can it do?" thought Raven. "He's already at death's door."

Raven tentatively filled the syringe with the medicine on the bedside cabinet, up to the marking on the syringe. Time ticking, pressure mounting. She swiftly injected the syringe into the vein in the patient's hand, squeezing gently.

The solution flowed in slowly, and as this happened, the patient's wounds healed visibly at an incredible speed. It was amazing to witness, and she was mesmerized. Bloody wounds became sealed, new and fresh skin appeared like a speeded up movie. She glanced at the timer, the minutes ticked. An idea hit her.

"Walker, fill the syringes!" Raven instructed.

"Good plan." Walker encouraged.

Diligently, the angel knight filled the syringes and had them ready by each bed. She rushed over to the second patient, repeating the procedure, pressing down softly. The saline like solution exited the syringe, entering the patient's bloodstream. Upon removing the empty syringe; she looked at a newly healed person! It was magical and transformative!

"How much time left?" barked Raven.

"Twelve minutes." came the answer.

"Brilliant, we can do this; let's move to the next one." Raven rushed optimistically.

"Right behind you!" Walker enthused.

Kindle and Lynk kept track of the time, Raven and Walker moved to the next patient, a ten-year-old girl whose face was covered with shrapnel wounds. The girl was writhing in pain and mental torment, enduring fear and hurt. Quick as lightning, Raven injected the girl. The little girl's face magically returned to its original state, and she slowly calmed as pain and fear changed to comfort and trust. The girl's smile warmed Raven's heart.

Raven leapt to the next patient, while Walker supported.

Raven injected a wounded boy. In seconds, the boy's wounded body returned to normal.

The next sufferer was a five-year-old boy. Upon reaching the boy, she found a spoon next to his bed, with the healing solution. She gently lifted his head and slowly coaxed the solution into his mouth, the boy swallowed it. She hurried onto the next person.

"Already, a third of them are healed," Raven muttered to Walker.

"That's efficiency, Raven."

"But we can't relax."

"How much time's left?"

"Eight minutes."

Dark Rise: The Nightmares' Isolation

"Perfect."

"You're not worried?"

"I am, but I'm trying to work within the limit."

Though slightly distracted, Raven quickly used the syringe, giving another patient the medicine, fascinated to see the patient's lacerations disappear, and new skin replace his wounds.

Raven began feeling powerful as a healer. She wished she could make this amazing healing solution to take with her when she returned home.

"Imagine how much suffering I could alleviate in the world. If only this was possible." she thought

Her confidence grew as she realized she could work fast and consistently, especially as she could see immediate healing results. It made her feel good; it made her feel useful; it made her feel intelligent, competent, powerful, and strong. She went on confidently to all the patients, giving them the necessary treatment, but now it was with a reassuring smile for them, and a comforting pat on the hand too.

In seeing their need, their injuries and pain, she forgot her own. She forgot that she was searching for her home and family. She immersed herself in giving care to others, giving reassurance, comfort, and help. She tended each patient as fast and as well as she could.

For all her efforts to help others, she was amazed at what she was receiving back. She found herself feeling thankful, that she was intelligent, and physically fit. Certainly, she felt luckier than those she was helping. The shift in her thinking was new and it made her grateful. How odd that she was putting all the effort into giving and healing, yet she felt better, as if she was being healed whilst she was helping others to recover. It confounded her, this paradigm, but also contented her. As her thought processes changed and her energy levels soared, she thought with a wry smile- *perhaps she would even be able to get the better of the whisperer.*

Whilst this situation appeared horrendous at first, she found, to her amazement and disbelief, good came with it, side by side! The healing of patients and removing suffering gave her joy in a bleak place. Although it was horrible to see terrible suffering and injuries, she came to enjoy seeing her patients getting better and the gratitude and smiles of her patients was just infectious, so she found herself smiling back and filling up with elation in spite of her situation. Her fear had temporarily all but disappeared whilst she was helping others.

"*Wow.*" thought Raven.

This experience taught Raven about herself, what she was capable of, what she enjoyed, and give meaning to her life. She wondered if she were ever to get home, whether a career in healing would be something that she could follow. Thoughts of home made her feel lonely but more determined to pass the tests to get there. Hopefully, the whisperer would keep his word, or it would be the ultimate deception-she wasn't sure if she could bare that, she knew he was the wrong entity to trust. But what choice did she have? She vowed to herself to keep her ears and eyes open to see if there were other ways forward. She did know she had a caring nature so loathed to hurt others, but desperation makes people do hateful things for self-preservation.

Sometimes it seemed life had thrown Raven so many hardships that good choices had become difficult, but where possible she would make the right choice. Her mind raced with self-reflection and new resolve.

As Raven finished healing the last patient, she moved forwards and inadvertently stepped on a large crack at the opposite end of the room. This happened so fast, she barely had a chance to prepare or react. She was now going down and she could do nothing to save herself.

At home, Amber wondered why the police hadn't found Raven. She looked across at her parents' faces drawn with silent distress, trying to hide their feelings from her, she too tried desperately to put a positive spin on the situation and said "she must be alive if they haven't found her, I'm sure she'll be back". The vacant seat at the dinner table made Amber feel empty. Amber didn't tell her parents that she was searching for Raven along with Sajid and Taz, trying to protect them from further worry. The lines of stress already etched on their faces. She feared that they would lose another daughter, thus keeping secrets protecting one another from further grief.

Fearing that Raven may have died in an accident or could have been injured, Amber went with Sajid and Taz and searched in the hospitals. On the way, Amber encountered Victoria and her close friends Robyn, Amy and Katherine.

"Hey, Amber, what are you doing out so late?" Victoria asked.

"I'm looking for Raven." Amber responded.

"Would you like us to help?" Victoria probed.

"No thanks, Victoria." Amber told her.

Amber walked quickly away from Victoria and her friends. She could feel Victoria's words were pretend and knew that she wasn't really intending to help."

"That Victoria is a snake." Amber shivered with distaste.

Victoria hungered for exultation and along with Robyn, Amy and Katherine, spread horrible rumors about Raven being dead. Victoria savored Raven's absence and hoped she wouldn't return anytime soon, she wanted to enjoy being head girl. Amber was no fool.

John Rahway

Chapter Ten

A Grateful Prayer

A loud thud rang out as Raven hit the ground, her hands, knees and elbows hurt upon collision. Disorientated, she dragged herself back up, the pain in her body was so great, and she could barely stand. However, she stabilized herself and managed to stand upright. Brushing herself down, she looked around and spotted Kindle, Walker and Lynk.

"Where are we?"

"We're in a jungle."

"It's amazing!"

"It sure is, Kindle, and we always seem to land somewhere unexpected, we never know if we're going to land somewhere nice or horrible."

"This place is incredible."

"It's nice to be outdoors surrounded by nature. The last realm felt a bit suffocating but this one feels like a breath of fresh air."

Drinking a small amount of her healing water, Raven surveyed her surroundings, a lush paradise, full of ancient ruins and thick green jungle landscapes. As she looked around, a wave of peace and relaxation washed over her.

As she relaxed, she began wandering, looking to satiate her hunger. Fortunately, there were a huge number of fruit trees and so a constant supply of food. However, branches and thorns made it difficult to get around. But she didn't mind for she had been in horrid situations, and thus far, this seemed very enjoyable.

Constantly wiping beads of sweat in the warmth and humidity, she reached for a golden apple; Kindle saw this, so with a strike of his beak he knocked the apple off. Raven caught it.

"Thanks, Kindle, this looks sweet."

"You're welcome, Raven."

Raven ate the apple ravenously, enjoying the sweet and juicy flesh. She heard a loud squawk coming from the trees ahead; a keel billed toucan flew into her path and she was mesmerized at its tameness and beauty.

Helping herself to fruits and berries, she noticed the jungle appeared serene and beautiful; it seemed quiet, too quiet.

Wondering about the uncanny silence, she found herself at the edge of a clear blue lagoon; it sent an eerie feeling into her bones. She felt regretful at being unable to relax and enjoy the natural beauty surrounding her; she loved animals, nature, and the landscape. Sadly though, her personal circumstances were fraught with fear and urgency. This compelled her into suspicion, of everything and everyone. She felt forced to be on high alert while traversing through these realms. She was on a quest to find her past, her family, and her friends. Her situation trapped her, especially with Mephistopheles manipulating and controlling her. *Could she be sure if she accomplished all that he had commanded, that he would honor his end of the deal.* She often worried that he may double cross her, after using her for his ends. After all, he was Mephistopheles, not to be trusted; deceit was synonymous with his name "Mephistopheles". With this thought, Raven decided to make the most of this tranquility, Mephistopheles would have to wait. So, she opted to sit down by the edge of the lagoon, rest and enjoy some of the fruits growing around. She took in the scenery and breathed a sigh of relief. If her premonitions were correct and something horrible were to occur, she decided she would cross that bridge when she came to it. Everything had been hectic, moving from one realm to another, always time pressure to complete the task and to get out in one piece. Her memories were in the hands of Mephistopheles and were being used to control her. She could not be sure that he would ever give them back. She had to trust the devil himself. She smiled ruefully and decided she would unwind, and rest a while; devil may care attitude-she thought reflectively.

As she rested, Raven thought about travelling from realm to realm. She often had to escape from treacherous and dangerous opponents.

"What is the purpose of each realm?" she thought. *"Is it to learn and grow? To be prepared for what lies ahead on this uncertain journey? Or to learn new skills? To become stronger, physically and mentally? Or to learn to problem solve?"*

Certainly, every realm was a new experience. She was becoming accustomed to the unusual, to the menacing, and the threatening. She had to use every skill within her being; of speed, resourcefulness and strength. Her traverse from realm to realm, time zone to time zone had changed her already; she was no longer the timid, shy, person that had started on this quest.

She mused, that whilst her situation was unusual it nevertheless bore similarities to the usual life a person lives. This thought brought some comfort. Her companions were very unusual; Kindle, an eagle, Walker, a broken angel knight and Lynk, Walker's Alaskan malamute. She was grateful for their presence, but she felt she was a puppet in Mephistopheles' control.

Wasn't everyone being controlled by something? Some people were controlled by their employers, having to work for someone else's prestige and profit, others by parents, schools or joyless jobs only to earn barely enough to survive. Yes, everybody was controlled and manipulated by somebody.

Relaxing by the lagoon, she was content momentarily, as she reflected that her situation wasn't that much worse than anyone else's. Everyone seemed to be gathering experiences to take to the Great Abyss-the unknown from where nobody has ever returned. Was death just another realm, or the end *of the ever-moving journey?*

Perhaps that's all life is; moving from realms, experiences and tests.

No one knows when they are born, how it will feel to come into the realm of life. There's the realm of babyhood with its dependency, its falls, discoveries and growth. It's a weak and helpless state, where you are at the mercy of others for protection, food and survival. There was the realm of childhood or youth, each realm was left behind. Each realm had its tests and triumphs then closed its doors and forbade return. As you move forward in life, the door to the past shuts itself on you. Similarly, no one has returned from the Great Abyss, life teaches its lessons and then bids you goodbye forever.

It seemed everyone had needed a few moments to rest and reflect.

Raven was feeling tempted to cross the lagoon. Its beauty beckoned. Kindle had just spotted a huge sea turtle.

"Perhaps we can cross on that sea turtle."

"Get on it."

"Yeah, but what if it knocks me off?"

"It won't harm you."

Raven hesitantly got onto the sea turtle's shell, with wobbly footsteps, her panic turned to excitement, for she was actually riding a sea turtle! Walker weightlessly leapt on with Lynk and the sea turtle swam with its surfers. Riding the sea turtle, made her feel connected with nature; it was exhilarating and wonderful at the same time. Eventually, they found themselves near a green bank and Raven reluctantly climbed off. Gratefully waving goodbye, she was enthralled by the natural beauty of the valley before her.

Luckily for Raven, she could run long distances, without tiring, thanks to her slim and athletic build. Running downhill made her feel she was flying towards the rip roaring waterfalls in the clearing.

"Wow, it's amazing how low we are now."

Even in her excitement, she could feel a premonition that something terrible was awaiting her.

Suddenly, the clouds above swelled and spat torrential rain.

"Quick, the land's sliding!"

Large black and red frogs with bulbous eyes croaked in unison; the rainfall intensified. The sodden ground started to break apart and fall into the lagoon.

Move quickly!" The land was disappearing into the water, slipping out from beneath her. This part of the lagoon was unnaturally colored but another turtle floated in front of her.

"Raven, get on the turtle."

"Ok, Kindle."

She leapt on with her companions

The sound of water shifting, and swirling attracted her attention and she noticed an enormous creature that resembled a goliath tigerfish with crimson red eyes following them.

"There's a huge fish here!!"

"Relax, Raven."

"Relax, how can I relax with this monster after us?" Raven screamed. "It's giving chase!"

It sailed over purposefully, viciously snapping at the sea turtle; eyes aflame. Its teeth missed only by a narrow margin.

"That was a close one!"

The monstrous fish missed the sea turtle, but lunged again. The turtle moved aside, but the predator's teeth scraped the turtle's left flipper, cutting it.

Blood flowed; the huge monster smelled it. Excited, it quickened its pace; the smell of blood enticed it. The fish snapped ferociously at the wounded turtle.

The beast targeted Raven; its huge head on the shell of the turtle. She turned around, knocking it back with a kick, and it vanished into the murky depths.

"That's him gone."

The turtle's flipper was bleeding. She glanced down, and there it was savagely attacking again!

"He's not giving up."

"Distract him"

Kindle swooped down and pecked at the huge fish.

The fish leapt at Kindle, shooting for him like a torpedo. Kindle disappeared! Panicked, her heart racing, she looked frantically, until, finally saw him flying ahead. She breathed a sigh of relief.

"Raven, aim your scythe at that tree, and blast it out."

"Make a tree barrier in the lagoon!"

A string of purple lightning flowed from the blade and ripped the tree from the grass, knocking it into the water with a heavy splash, blocking the goliath tigerfish's path!

Raven's heart skipped a beat when she heard the thunderous crash. Tree bark flew up into the sky like an exploding firework, and when she looked back, she saw that the fish was stunned and hemmed in by the large tree trunk. It was unharmed and still had its freedom; it just couldn't reach Raven and the turtle for now.

As Raven looked at the fish, she spotted a skull shaped badge.

"Kindle, do you know what that is, on the fish's head?"

"Yes, it's a devil symbol."

Raven dismounted the turtle and applied some healing water on its injury. She then turned her attention to the symbol on the tigerfish's head and aimed her scythe at it, a narrow stream of electricity shot from the blade and burned the symbol to cinders.

Without this symbol, the fish's eyes returned from red to silver. This shocked Raven, and she realized that the fish had been under Mephistopheles' influence.

Freed from this control, the fish had a soft gentle demeanor. Raven stood still, puzzled.

Some instinct within Raven overrode her fear and compelled her to allow the beast to approach her. It seemed like madness but she hoped she was making a good decision.

"Thank you for freeing me from Mephistopheles' curse, I wish you success in your quest and that you meet kind souls like yourself."

Raven was touched and she smiled gratefully.

"Thank you."

After thanking Raven and wishing her well on her journey the monstrous fish turned and dived deep into the lagoon. It had reminded her that she too was under Mephistopheles' control as she searched for her family. Mephistopheles apparently had the key.

Raven wistfully turned and followed Walker's lead towards the light ahead. "I have an affinity with animals, and I can quite often understand their thoughts and motives for doing something and he was being compelled to do what he did."

"True but he still tried to kill you."

The light beckoned and was pulling her in. It was so enticing that her encounter with the fish was leaving her mind.

As she looked at the light, Raven hoped it would lead to something pleasant.

"I wonder if we're travelling in time this time."

"Kindle, you don't seem your usual self, is everything ok?"

"Don't worry, Raven, I'm ok."

"No, Kindle, something's wrong."

"I hurt my head when I was wrestling the fish."

"Why don't you try a sip of my water?"

After Raven gave Kindle a tiny sip of her water, healing began, and his brain regenerated. Gratefully, he took flight ahead of Raven and she followed him enthusiastically. Legs light and quick; her mind fixed on the goal. Kindle led her to where the light was beckoning; she thought the light might be a step closer to attaining what she needed. But one thing was for sure, whatever she found she would keep it to herself. The light lifted Raven's spirits and heightened her sense of adventure.

At school, Amber couldn't concentrate on the lessons at all. She dreamed and focused on Raven, wondering when her sister would return. She spent lessons planning where to search next. When school was finished, Amber readied Taz, their Alsatian, and continued their search for Raven, this time they searched in the woods nearby where she and Raven used to play together as children.

John Rahway

Chapter Eleven

A Feast For Sharks

Following the light led her into a new realm. Raven felt alert, her brain thinking fast but then she suddenly remembered that Walker was working for Mephistopheles!

"So you're working for the one blackmailing and manipulating me?" asked Raven. "So you're in on it! Do you know my family?"

Walker hesitated before he answered. "I'm just here to support you through this journey."

"How can I trust you?" Raven fired back.

Walker's pause before answering made her feel he was hiding something.

"Can you help me get back to my family, Walker?" Raven pleaded softly.

Walker's loyalty was divided, he said "I'll try my best, Raven."

Raven was convinced that Walker knew more than he was saying. But there was no time to get any more information from him, as they were disturbed by a shrill voice saying "Welcome to a world of irrepressible anger and sorrow."

"Who said that?" snarled Raven, looking round rapidly, "Come on, show yourself!"

She appeared, a small, crippled, and hunched over old woman with tightly closed sightless eyes. The old woman was holding a wooden staff in her right hand.

"So, I have to fight you, to get out of here?" asked Raven fiercely.

"No, you will not fight me, but you will endure a battle against your emotions." The old woman replied.

Suddenly, the old woman pointed her staff at Raven, locking onto her mind. Sharp pain shot through her head as she seemed to lose control over her mind.

"What's going on?" asked Raven. Her mind took her through a series of visions. Each vision showed different sorrowful incidents and her eyes began to burn.

"Just look in front of you." said the old woman.

Raven curiously followed the old woman's instruction; her sightless visage was fixed on the horizon. Raven saw the ground in front changing to sea water. She looked up and saw a huge ocean liner creep into her eye line. The cabin and rudder of a submarine protruding like a shark's fin also emerged from the depths. Raven beheld an entire fleet of fishing boats, with nets full of fish and cruel fishermen severing the fins of sharks before cruelly dumping them back into the ocean for them to die slowly and painfully. She witnessed them writhing in pain as they tried in vain to swim away, leaving a trail of blood. A senseless cruelty, a misuse of power, money making through abuse; her helplessness squeezed her heart. Raven stood still, thinking fast. Although, she was now used to strange occurrences happening all the time, she was uncertain if she was dreaming or really living these experiences.

"How will a body of sea water, an ocean liner and a submarine test my emotions?" smiled Raven.

The old, sightless woman inexplicably pointed at the ocean liner and submarine; this was when Raven looked at it properly. She saw that the ocean liner was directly in the path of the speeding submarine.

"Seriously, what's so special about these ships?" Raven started to ask. "Oh no!"As realization dawned.

She heard Walker's voice whispering calmly, "fear is only your imagination and your subconscious scaring you."

Suddenly, a huge torpedo shot out from the water, slicing the ocean liner into sinking sections, with an explosion, causing her to jump as an enormous blazing red-orange fireball flooded the water. The explosion cleared, Raven looked at the carnage; she saw thousands of men, women, and children, helplessly flailing about in the water.

Raven clasped her hands over her mouth, at their desperate situation as they tried to swim to safety. Their fright and panic seared her. But this was only the beginning. For now, hundreds of triangles appeared in the sea.

Some deep metallic indigo blue; others bronze tipped with mottled white; a large number were dark grey, and the remainder olive green. Seconds after appearing, one of the deep metallic blue triangles shot towards the people, moving at terrific speed, sleek, powerful, ruthless, and propelled by a powerful tail. Food!

Terrified screams of pain pierced the air, as copious amounts of blood merged with the water. Raven saw the cold, cruel eyes of a shortfin mako shark fixated on its prey. It renewed its attack, teeth bared, eyes glinting, it ripped flesh.

As Raven saw red in the water, she felt repulsed, as a sharp pain shot into her throat, constricting her breath. She breathed harshly, trying her best to suppress the raw emotion.

She longed to close her eyes but dared not as an oceanic whitetip shark tore at someone's legs. The whitetip then devoured the already dead person.

"What's the matter, child?" the old woman said in a tone of mock comfort

"Well, this is a horrific scene; it's terrible to see such pain and suffering." Raven answered.

"There's no point fighting against your emotions, for they will overcome you." Raven heard the old woman hissing.

"You can't not feel sympathy or empathy for these people." Raven stated.

Raven knelt down silently, linking her fingers together. In this humble and pleading posture, she shut her eyes, bowed her head, and prayed.

While Raven beseeched silently, the old woman sensed she was praying. Though unable to see, the mystic's other senses were heightened, and she could feel the emotion Raven was going through. Through her prayer Raven found inner calm. She was able to tune into her inner senses, see the situation clearly and focus on stilling herself, whilst seeking solutions that her conscious mind could not solve. Luckily; her deep sub conscious mind gave her clarity. The quiet otherworldliness of a metaphysical connection enabled this for her. She found inner peace and calm to deal with her surroundings.

"I see you're a mystic." said Raven.

"Well done, you're catching on." The mystic said coolly.

The mystic angered her but Raven fought to neutralize the negative emotions that were trying to burn up inside her. As she opened her eyes, and saw the ongoing violence in the water.

She felt accosted by the devastation. However, her prayer had helped her to realize that it was all an illusion designed for fear mongering; like a horror movie. She saw the fishermen trying to get close to rescue the people in the water amongst the fire, the fuel and sharks.

With a flash of its teeth, a smooth hammerhead shark tore into someone and another body entered a watery grave. Blood gushed, enticing more sharks to feast. Sure enough, a shiver of tiger sharks sailed in.

Raven didn't know how to help, how to make this bloodbath stop.

Through concealed tears, Raven bowed her head.

"Please, Zirnitra great Slavic dragon God of sorcery, stop the bloodshed, stop the hatred, let peace resume, grant me the strength to control my emotions. Enable me to stay strong." Raven prayed.

Raven's lack of emotion frustrated the old mystic; so she struck her with her stick. Annoyed at being hit unnecessarily, Raven turned around; wanting to lash out but with great self-control, maintained her calm, knowing she was hit for provocation.

"Do you really think prayer will help you?" the mystic asked mockingly.

Raven connected silently, ignoring the mystic, hoping for peace and strength. As she did so, she opened her eyes, still sparkling with unshed tears, only to witness a terrifying yet mesmerizing sight. A shortfin mako shark leapt from the water with a body in its mouth and with one swing of its powerful head, the shark disappeared with it.

"Oh my." Raven gasped.

"That's right let your shock and fear rise." The mystic bullied.

Raven breathed in sharply to suppress her anger and sadness, fighting to maintain composure. The tears were begging to come out; her heart thudded violently, witnessing an oceanic whitetip shark tearing flesh. *"Whilst it is in the nature of wild beasts to prey, the so-called circle of life"* she couldn't condone the action of men blowing up the ship needlessly, leading to savage loss of life. This, she found unforgiveable, for man is a creature that has a brain to reason and judge right from wrong. Manmade destruction and brutality were incomprehensible. The sharks were simply feasting on the plentiful supply of unexpected food that appeared in their habitat.

The mystic was cruel and gleeful as Raven witnessed these horrific scenes, hoping for Raven to lose the battle with her emotions.

Raven used meditation to strengthen her from fear but also to safeguard against her own anger towards the mystic, whilst protecting her from the sadness of the scene in the water. Her upper lip wobbled; her eyes burned from the sorrow that was trying to brim over. Fear of satisfying the mystic was keeping the tears back; as she knew she could be trapped in this realm.

"Raven, stay strong, you're doing really well." Walker encouraged.

"What's going on, why aren't you reacting?" the mystic goaded. "I can sense your tears."

"I know that, but I'll not cry in front of you." Raven retorted bravely. A few people had swum to the fishing boats.

Suddenly, the tears faded from Raven's eyes, along with the fear in her heart, despite the shark attacks. Raven remained composed, new strength flowing through her. Her refocus made her realize that her purity of heart and compassion was stronger than her anger.

Suddenly, a vicious wind blew towards the mystic; the cold sliced her like a thousand knives. Deep bloody cuts appeared all over her body as she shrieked in pain.

"Where is that wind coming from?" the mystic screamed.

"The wind above is the answer to my prayer." Raven said firmly.

"B-b-but you're an idolatress." The mystic howled.

"I am, but that doesn't mean my petition for an end to this cruelty and bloodshed is overlooked." Raven retorted.

"What's happening, why am I being cut, and why am I bleeding?" shrieked the mystic.

"What the sharks have done to the people in the water is what they're going to do to you." Raven stated.

The mystic yelled in horror, at the thought of being torn apart, by the very sharks that she had made Raven witness.

Raven stood at her full height, staring at the mystic who had mentally abused her, and the sharks, that would consume her. The mystic turned around, trying in vain to flee her impending doom. However, it wasn't to be, for the wind blew and a splash hit the water and a scream was heard.

Raven turned, brushed a tear and moved on.

Amber hoped Raven was all right wherever she was. She and Taz searched the beaches, they scanned every face they saw there in the hopes that Raven would be there. She saw many ships on the water, thinking that perhaps Raven would be on one.

Dark Rise: The Nightmares' Isolation

Chapter Twelve

Qagloucian Blaze

Stepping through the gap, Raven looked around. The environment looked calm with quaint little avenues, tree lined and bordered by flowering bushes. It looked very ordinary, very pleasant. She would take her time to reflect and collect her thoughts, rest a little and enjoy some down time, she knew as always it was the calm before the storm. Raven reflected as to what was expected of her in this realm, it just seemed to be test after test. Sometimes it helped her focus when she knew what the requirements were. She knew it was about controlling emotions in the last realm, but she didn't know what to expect here. What would she do with all these skills she was amassing on route?-maybe it was going to be useful for a bigger challenge, hidden in the secret vault of time, that might unfold one day. But whatever was in store, she knew that the past was out of reach for her, the doors slammed shut! Her quest was about finding her family and her memories. She yearned to go back into the past. The future was also out of reach, she had no idea what tomorrow held, would tomorrow bring her family to her? She hoped her future would be with friends and family. How she wished so! After these experiences, would the future be mundane? Would she find it boring because she had been through some frightening, adrenaline fueled experiences which were changing her? But what she knew for certain was that hidden amongst the lost past and mysterious future all she had was now! Now was her present and she had to make it worthwhile, successful, and pleasant. Ironically every exit led to another enclosure, another world fraught with trials where she was tested to the limit.

Raven knew that she had to keep learning and evolving. Time stood still for no one; it kept shifting and changing the circumstances. Everyone was a prisoner of time, trapped in their own time troubles. She had to make the most of now! Just as she didn't always find what she needed after every exit, tomorrow may not bring all that she wanted either. She would just have to play the hand that she was dealt, but resolved to enjoy and learn from it.

She would resolutely enjoy her companions of today, Kindle, Walker and Lynk, for they were with her through thick and thin and had been supportive, and protective; often having to forgive her outbursts. Raven may not have chosen them, but she had grown to love and respect them, but she was still a little uncertain of her friendship with Walker. So she decided to test it.

"Walker, do I have a family?" asked Raven. "Is anyone yearning for me while I'm searching for them?"

Walker hesitated and said awkwardly, "Once you've found what Mephistopheles is looking for I'm assured you'll be able to go free and find your family."

"That's not the answer to my question." snapped Raven. "So, where is my family, Walker? You know, don't you?"

A smell of smoke wafted through the air, its suffocating odor distracted Raven from her probing. She initially thought it a bonfire from someone's back garden. However, the ancient Qagloucian street became alive with commotion; people ran and screamed with terror. Raven anxiously observed the scorching flames licking houses and streets.

"Raven, the whole town is in danger." Kindle stated.

"We've got to find the source of the fire and destroy it." "Kindle, check out the area" Raven instructed.

Kindle spread his wings, effortlessly flying ahead, watching for danger, while Raven, Walker and Lynk followed below. As Kindle flew, he saw a great hill far in the distance, with a medieval castle, surrounded by armored Qagloucian soldiers, guarding it. Suddenly, a blazing ball of debris flew towards Kindle, like a flaming comet.

"Kindle, watch out!"

"I'm ok, Raven."

Just as the burning debris shot forwards, Kindle swiftly steered out of its path, narrowly escaping a fiery death. However, the fire hit another house, with a sickening boom; smoke erupted from its roof.

"Kindle; do you know where the fire's coming from?"

"Raven, I hate to break it to you, but see that castle ahead? Someone's got a mechanical catapult and is using it to shoot fireballs into the town. From what I've seen it's a man named Hardegin who has owns the castle."

"Good grief, don't tell me that someone's starting it."

"I'm afraid so."

"Well let's not deliberate, it's the perfect time for a search and eliminate mission, what do you think?"

"Sounds fair, I look forward to breaking those mechanical catapults."

"I'm up for a little search and destroy as well."

"Good, let's make haste, shall we?"

"I'll take the lead."

"You're already ahead, Kindle."

"Oh yeah, I am." Laughed Kindle.

Raven followed Kindle below, watching as the eagle evaded fireballs. Anger filled Raven, and rage flashed in her eyes, as another fireball shot towards her.

"That's it, your fire ends here, and it ends now."

"Who are you saying that to, Raven?"

"The people who're setting fire to the place."

"They can't hear you, and we're too far away."

As Raven sped through the burning Qagloucia, she could hear the sound of fiddle play and a drunken singing voice. With incredulity, Raven said

"This place is on fire, and someone sits around singing, while playing the lyre, what a waste."

"Raven, use your energy to focus on destroying the source?"

"That's where we're headed."

Watching for fireballs, Raven saw a child's parents set alight, while the child ran away terrified. Horrified, she used her scythe and projected a cold blast towards them and found it put the flames out over the couple, who quickly ran on to join their child. But sadly, it didn't have enough power to put all the flames out, she aimed it at other people who were caught alight, and it gave them a bit more time to escape. She put out what she could.

As more fireballs were flung, Raven moved swiftly, evading them with precision and care. The inferno roared like an enraged dragon, consuming the inhabitants of the houses.

"I swear I'll stop this madman."

"Raven, stop making promises you can't keep."

"I'll bring him to justice."

An irate Raven sped like lightning. Her heart blazed with fury, as she promised to bring about the downfall of Hardegin.

Simultaneously, two fireballs shot forwards, the power from Raven's scythe deflected them to fall into a nearby river, where they fizzled out on contact.

"Nice one, Raven."

"Your scythe is clearly extraordinary."

"You're definitely right, but I'm worried about getting up the hill, into the castle without being caught?"

"We're nearly there; I have a bird's eye view."

Mansonee Hill was shrouded by trees and bushes; great cover for a slight girl to hide in as she crept up following the sound of the lyre.

"Walker, you're really not helping at the moment, have you got a plan."

"So, I have to come up with the plan?"

"Oh really, you've made it up to this area, and you don't know what to do?"

"I don't, so what should we do?"

"How should I know?"

Amidst the carnage, Raven registered that she and her friends were bickering! She knew she should put a stop to it but couldn't help answering back and fanning more flames of disagreement. She kicked herself, but her ego got in the way again as she retorted back.

"Wait a minute, arguing won't solve anything, and we need to work out a plan."

"I'm with you on that, Raven."

"I'll be happy to help."

Raven was pleasantly surprised to see how easily she managed to conclude the arguing. She exercised self-control, and smiled to herself as everyone started to discuss options.

Aside from the soldiers pulling the catapults, there are soldiers guarding the castle, how shall we go about dealing with them?"

After making amends with Kindle, Raven carried on following his lead, whilst the horrible odor of smoke and ash wafted through the air.

"I'm looking forward to getting rid of Hardegin, his tyranny and his worthless toy."

"I agree, what kind of madman sets his empire on fire?" Walker agreed.

"Sadly, some people are just tyrants, they are unfair and unkind."

In a much better mood, Raven began to pick up the pace while a smile lit her eyes. She focused her thoughts on removing Hardegin from power and began running behind Kindle.

"You've perked up, Raven."

"Let's just say, I have an intention to stop Hardegin's violence, I don't know how, but I mean to try. But if we can put the soldiers to sleep, then we should be able to walk in. Kindle, can you fly by and see where we can get sleeping grenades from?" Raven directed.

"Good plan!" Kindle agreed.

"Walker, you're an angel, you probably know what people are keeping where, because you can see anywhere and go wherever you want to go, let's use your powers from now on."

"Cut into the hill, I can see a weapons' storage." Kindle informed them.

"Walker, you have the gift of invisibility, see if you can get into the weapons storage and bring back something to put the guards to sleep with." Raven instructed.

Excited by her plan, Raven kept in the shadows, whilst climbing the hill. Leaving devastation behind, her anger added a flash of fuel to her motivation. She wandered to herself about what qualities a leader should have. Fairness, justice and using power to benefit everybody, rather than to just sit around and use real people as entertainment; the game Hardegin was playing! Leaders, rulers, and people in power need to be compassionate and have empathy for others. They need to understand their problems, and life goals. To achieve that, one must meet people of all classes, colors, and faiths, understand them, care for them, and motivate them to succeed.

She suspected that Hardegin had never met or cared for anyone. He seemed over privileged and a psychopath, or he would not be hurting people.

Raven wondered what was required of her, *was it to remove him from power and find a replacement. No the townspeople would have to choose their own elected leader; someone who would try to help people, a just and compassionate ruler. She wondered how much was expected of her.*

Feeling a little acrophobic, on the ascent, she had to swallow her fear, and summon up the courage to face her enemy. Too much was at stake.

Walker led her to the ammunition store.

"Raven, you need to pick up the sleeping grenades."

Upon reading the instructions on the grenade, she learned that upon contact with the ground, it released gas that knocked anything in the area unconscious. Raven's eyes narrowed and her smile became more sinister.

"Ready to put Hardegin away, guys?"

"I sure am."

"Let's knock him off his high horse."

"I'd love to jump on him." The Malamute chimed in.

Adrenaline energized Raven now she had the sleeping gas grenades. Raven's ears were filled with Emperor Hardegin's annoying lyre playing and she followed the sound.

Suddenly, Raven heard a shout from above. She looked up and saw Hardegin's guards pointing at her.

"Emperor, there's a girl coming up the hill."

"Not to worry, Wimpacus, she will not get past the sentries. Guards, go and deal with the intruder."

"Yes, Emperor Hardegin."

All the guards, save for Wimpacus, ran down the hill with their swords and spears glinting in the sun. Raven stood still, watching carefully for the right moment, or her efforts would be useless. Before long, the guards were near; taken aback it was just a lone girl.

Raven knew it was now or never. She donned a protective mask, hid herself, took a few steps back and used one of Hardegin's own catapults she had found in his weapons' store to fire the grenades at them. The grenades soundlessly hit the ground, and green fumes filled the air.

"Hope you like the taste of your own medicine, Hardegin."

The guards inhaled the gas and fell to the ground. The guards unconscious, Raven raised her scythe, using the lightning to dissipate the gas, while swiftly running up the hill.

A path cleared in the gas, Raven marched to stay close to Kindle, in order to storm the castle. She watched and listened for Hardegin's singing and fireballs. No singing could be heard, for Hardegin was sound asleep, snoring. The grenades had done their job.

Raven was determined to end the dictatorship. With everyone asleep, it was child's play to enter the castle. She made her way to where Hardegin was sleeping. She saw beautiful ornate rooms and opulence, and there he was living an undeserved life of luxury. Raven struggled to think of how best to rid the people of this man.

She planned to end these people's ordeal! With Wimpacus and all the guards snoring, she sheathed her scythe and sought an exit. Raven panicked, for there were no doors that led beyond other rooms in the castle.

"Walker, Kindle, Lynk, can you help me find an exit, as it's time to leave this place and get rid of Hardegin."

As they searched before the guards could wake, Lynk began to paw at the bookshelf.

Curious to see what Lynk was pawing at, Raven went to the bookshelf and pushed it and to her surprise it revealed a passage beyond the castle. Realizing that there was a way through the moving bookshelf, she decided with Walker to drag Hardegin towards it as she could see this was indeed the way out from this realm. She intended that Hardegin would also lose his power and luxury, but she wasn't going to kill him! She wasn't going to soil herself with his blood. No, she would take him with her! This was how she would eliminate his tyranny.

"Let's see how powerful he is without all his guards to help him in his vicious, self centered plan."

The bookshelf spun back into place, forbidding return.

Amber's heartbreak and grief over Raven was always present, at home and at school. Her studies suffered as she focused on her sister's whereabouts. She prayed anxiously for Raven's safe return. She and Taz searched the parks where she and Raven had played together, trying to find a sign of her sister.

John Rahway

Chapter Thirteen

Athaenian Plague

With the fire now behind her, Raven surveyed the new setting. She was standing in a garden filled with flowering plants and bushes; in the gardens of a huge Athaenian castle. As she curiously looked around, she saw Hardegin was stirring, semi awake, rubbing his eyes looking around, stupefied. She grinned to herself as she watched him.

"Not so powerful now, your majesty." she said out loud, "without your guards and soldiers you're a bit of a wimp like all bullies. Hopefully, this experience will teach you to be a nice normal person."

Raven found it thoroughly entertaining watching him come to his senses, not sure where he was, and Kindle, Walker and Lynk all looked amused by this spectacle. Hardegin looked helpless, such a contrast! Hard hearted Hardegin was now helpless Hardegin.

"Bullies like him don't know when life will change." Thought Raven.

All, that had taken was a move to another location to completely change his behavior, his outlook on life and to safeguard those he had tyrannized.

"He's now going to have to start over again." She mused as Kindle flew on to her shoulder. If this worked for Hardegin who was a hardened criminal, Raven thought, this could work for young first-time offenders who could work out their sentence by working, learning and training in different locations away from toxic influences. This could save them from a life of crime and regret.

"This garden seems so beautiful and peaceful." said Raven.

"True but looks can be deceiving." Walker responded.

"I worry that this peace may become a nightmare as it's often been the case in my experience." Raven added.

"Let's look on the bright side hopefully all will go well, for now let's just enjoy the beauty of the gardens." Kindle interjected.

The castle gardens were immense, and Raven could see they had been lovingly tended with great regard and respect for nature. There were orange trees, pomegranate, lemon, olive, apricot, peach and cherry trees and herbs such as mint, basil, rosemary amongst flower borders of roses, and bougainvillea. Nestled amongst these were bug hotels, to encourage pollination and aphid control; natural ways to control pests including Venus fly traps and pitcher plants. These devoured insects for lunch. In addition to the fruit orchards there were also vegetable beds containing tomatoes, courgettes, aubergines, sweetcorn, beetroot, strawberries, raspberries, and blueberries. There were many plants that encouraged birds such as magpies, woodpeckers, starlings, and swallows.

Raven's legs started to flag. Her breathing became labored, and she felt faint. At this point she decided to prioritize her health. She realized without her health and wellbeing, she could do nothing to help others and she crumpled down against a tree.

Walker brought her some food and drink, which she ate and washed it down with fruit juice. Slowly, her energy returned as she rested and reflected. She was grateful to Walker for his prompt caring and concern, she realized if she didn't take care of herself-she could become ill and then her quest to find her past, would just be a futile dream. At this point she decided not to be a hero, let Mephistopheles wait!

She mischievously smirked at the thought of him being frustrated waiting for his precious gems.

"*Stuff him.*" thought Raven.

On humanitarian grounds, Raven would help people against Mephistopheles' plots and harms when she could but after making sure she was well first. At this point, she decided to take care to seek out nourishment while exercising her brain and all muscle groups so she could increase her strength. Without energy or power, she would be useless against a strong enemy, her body and brain would shut down and that could be the end.

A buzzing sound interrupted her train of thought. Listening carefully, trying to figure out what it was, Raven looked around, her eyes alert. She saw a few wasps and relaxed again.

Not long after, swarms of wasps flew in like military jets. Raven's heart jumped, and she barely had a chance to react, let alone fend them off. She moved, evading the swarm as they flew.

"Wasps! This is Mephistopheles' doing!" Raven snapped.

"Raven, I know you're annoyed, but you're making assumptions." Walker reminded her.

Raven, feeling irritated, inspected the wasps feeding off the leaves and flowers. To her horror more and more seemed to be gathering. It was beginning to pose a serious problem.

Mischievously, she decided to delegate this to Hardegin; after all, he was used to sending fireballs at people so he could make himself useful and smoke them out! Not dissimilar to Hardegin, a wasp on its own was small and helpless, but an entire swarm could cause serious damage. The once powerful Hardegin was wandering around lost, slapping himself every time a wasp landed on him. Despite her wasp anxieties, every time she saw Hardegin, weak and pathetic, Raven felt a sense of satisfaction, and she grinned as she watched him cutting a comical figure, scared of little wasps without his guards and servants.

With a desire for self-protection, she forged forward, evading the increasing swarms. She was scanning for the source of the wasps and something to eliminate them with.

Raven's heart thumped as the swarm covered everything. She felt a bit sick, as the dark swarm flooded the place.

Raven forced herself to press on, motivated by solving the wasp problem ecologically without destruction.

Wasps were buzzing down, feasting hungrily. Some of them were flying at her.

"Why are they attacking me?" Raven asked fretfully

"Raven, stay calm, they'll get off if you stay calm." Walker advised.

"Walker, you're one to talk, how you know that?" asked Raven.

"I was once like you, Raven because when I was a human, I had to film some of my movies and do some of my charity works in hot countries and boy did the wasps attack, so if you freak out, more will come towards you but if you stay calm, they'll leave you." Walker explained.

Raven fought to stay calm and patient, though the wasps stayed put for a while. Eventually, they began to fly away from her, buzzing.

"Well let's look for something to get rid of the wasps." Walker suggested.

"I have a better idea, let Hardegin deal with it, as it is; the wasps are driving him mad." Raven couldn't help laughing at Hardegin's expense. "Kindle, can you try and spot for an exit, I'll see if I can find anything to eliminate the wasps."

"I'll see what I can do, Raven." Kindle replied.

"Thanks, Kindle." Said Raven.

Kindle flew fast and high, dodged wasps and scanned, his powerful wings sailed the air current. Raven, with Walker's help, searched for ideas to get rid of the wasps. His sharp eyes were searching, as he flew, and in seconds he located something in the distance.

"What can you see, Kindle?" asked Raven.

"It looks like there's a natural remedy for the wasp population. There are many bug hotels amongst the shrubbery including praying mantises, Raven, they feast on wasps, and it will help to control the wasp numbers, let's just wake them up and stir them into action, hopefully they can enjoy a feast." Kindle explained.

"Good idea." said Raven.

Raven walked towards the praying mantis habitats. She had mixed thoughts and felt squeamish about letting them out to feast on the wasp swarm. At the same time, she knew it had to be done; nature had to take its course. She felt it was releasing another swarm and it horrified her to think of the air thick with insects warring with each other. Self-preservation made her exercise her power of delegation and gave the job to Walker.

Raven swiftly removed herself from the vicinity of the bug hotels and observed from a safe vantage point. She watched as the feeding frenzy began and the wasp numbers started to decline.

"Kindle, do you think you can invite the bird population for a banquet?" asked Raven. "This might help the circle of life a bit more."

Kindle let out a screech and birds listened tentatively, came close and watched from a distance with heads cocked. A few took up the invitation and began feasting. Some of them sang and invited others of their own flocks to feed. Raven watched from a distance, glad to be hidden away from this feeding frenzy. She was pleased that she had used a natural method to control the wasps, rather than killing them indiscriminately. The thought occurred to her that, the wasps were important for pest control and ideally it would be better if they dispersed through the land to eat up the pests on crops growing on farms. With this realization she kick started the sprinkler system. The effect was spectacular; the wasps flew away to avoid the water, dispersing far and wide, to fulfill their purpose and do their natural job. She smiled knowing that she had preserved the food chain. She felt herself slowly gaining the upper hand on Mephistopheles.

Moving away from the insect frenzy, her mind returned to her own departure from this place. She needed to know that she could leave anytime she wished. It gave her a sense of freedom to know a way out.

"Raven, what's up?"

"Have you found an exit?"

"I think so but it's a big deep hole and I'm not sure how safe it is"

Walking to the tunnel, the sheer drop filled her stomach with butterflies and her body shook with fear.

"Raven, what are you waiting for, there's an exit below you."

"I can see that but it looks dangerous."

Raven positioned herself above the hole, her heart pounded as she moved. However, she didn't do anything.

"What's wrong, Raven." Asked Kindle

"Shall I go first or will you, Walker or Lynk?" Raven asked anxiously.

"You go."

"I'm frightened, Kindle, if you go first and return to warn me of what lies ahead that will help me immensely."

"Ok, Raven."

Kindle flew down the tunnel and assessed it before reporting back.

"Raven, the tunnel's smooth and it's like a slide and there are no obstacles beneath it and it should be safe."

After inhaling and exhaling deeply, Raven sat down nervously on the edge of the hole. She placed her arms over her body, before *adjusting* her legs to fall. In seconds, she shot down the hole. For a split second, her thoughts flashed across her mind, *"It might be safe for Kindle but is it safe for humans?"*

But Kindle had not ever given her any reason to distrust him.

Raven could barely see a thing, as her body flew through the tunnel. She shut her eyes tightly, to relax herself as she began shooting through. She hurtled through the claustrophobic tube, constructed from smooth stone. She could feel the cold stone rubbing against her cloak. Her shoulders ached from contacting the stone, she opened her eyes momentarily and could see the dark roof of the tube but an optimistic light lay at the bottom.

Suddenly, a gust of hot wind shot down, sending Raven forward fast. She couldn't react, because of the force. In seconds, she was zipping down as fast as a fighter jet, gasping for air as she sped.

As she zoomed down the tube, her senses were heightened by each passing second. The speed and velocity, at which she was travelling, increased violently and she was flung down, with barely enough time to react. Finally submitting to her predicament, she started to feel thrilled as if she was riding a roller coaster, so she decided to relax and enjoy the ride and hope for the best. Even through the excitement, Raven silently prayed for a safe landing.

The light increased in size. She was nearing the end of the tunnel.

Close to the end, she could hear Mephistopheles' taunting voice in her head.

"That's right, Raven, allow yourself to relax and sleep, I can see that you are tired." Mephistopheles whispered.

"Shut up, Mephistopheles, you're not going to get in my way." Raven snarled back.

"That's no way to talk to the one who will give you your memories back."

"Say what you like, besides, you only said you would do that if I got you the six precious gems."

"It's alright, Raven, I was only trying to test you to see whether you would sleep, but I'm pleased to tell you've passed the test."

Gritting her teeth in firm resolve, ignoring his voice, she hurtled out into the sunshine.

Raven opened her eyes and let the warm sunshine soothe away her aches and pains as she lay on the floor in a heap. She lay there, shell shocked for a while, warmed by the sun, hugely relieved. The sunshine restored her optimism and energy. She was becoming more confident. As she remembered her retort to Mephistopheles, she grinned because she had stood up to him. She was becoming less afraid of him and was managing to reduce his grip on her.

Amber held onto a strong hope that Raven was out there somewhere. Her hope kept her searching.

John Rahway

Chapter Fourteen

The Unbound Hurricane

S truggling to her feet with her head spinning. Raven looked around this new environment; she was standing in a coastal area where the weather felt erratic. However, the quiet tied her stomach in knots, as she was slightly anxious despite the relief.

She finally took a sip of water and felt better immediately.

Suddenly, Kindle emerged from the tube, with Walker and Lynk behind him. A wave of relief washed over Raven, though her heart was still on high alert. It was nice not to be alone, she was grateful as always to have Kindle, Walker and Lynk with her. Their company removed her anxiety, replacing it with optimism and vigor.

"Now that we're all here, we might as well explore."

"Good plan, Raven."

"I'll fly ahead."

However, before Kindle could do so, a powerful gust of wind shot towards him.

"Kindle, ride the wind."

"Sure thing, Raven."

Upon hearing Raven's instruction, Kindle raised his wings and soared up over the gust. Raven followed close behind, basking in the breeze. It was getting windier! She found the wind energizing and exhilarating! She stood to enjoy it and breathed deeply! It was so pleasant, so thrilling as it fanned her hair and blew her clothes about. It was the air of life itself! She loved it. She laughed aloud as she felt intoxicated by its freshness. She wanted to soak up its energy! Walker handed her a kite and they both laughed as the kites competed to reach the highest zenith. Her kite, a myriad of colors with an R emblazoned on it. The wind took it high, higher still; she had never been able to fly her kite this high before, it was such fun. Then all of a sudden the wind whipped it away and it was gone. It seemed to her that life was full of opposites. With every hardship there was also ease and with every ease there was a price to pay. Her days seemed to be full of beauty, peace, soothing breezes and then angry hurricanes. Opposites again, like night and day, pleasure and pain. No sooner had she thought this, the wind picked up speed–it no longer felt pleasant as it no longer caressed her face but slapped it instead. Her hair and clothes were out of control now. She headed for shelter!

Suddenly, a small tree was uprooted from the ground, it shot forward like an express train. Raven didn't duck but she drew out her scythe, swinging it diagonally and slicing the tree into bits.

"Wow that was dangerous."

"*I love this wind, but anything in excess is destructive,*" thought Raven. "*Wouldn't it be brilliant if we could master the wind, control it, and get it to do what we wanted? We could be so powerful with the wind on our side, it's the wind that pushes the clouds and brings the rain that grows everything and brings beauty and prosperity to the land and everyone benefits from it, yes I'd love to master the wind.*" thought Raven "*I'd be so powerful and in control, everyone would be coming to me to ask for rain to grow their crops or to stop the rain when they've had enough. I could ask for a cool breeze on a hot summer's day or to fan fresh air for feeling alive or get the wind to bring the rain and enrich the parched plants.*" she reflected.

As Raven followed Kindle, she looked around the area, noticing the damage and force of the hurricane. People ran, trying in vain to escape the fury of the wind as it picked up speed. Raven couldn't help feeling a spark of pity, wishing that she could help them.

However, Raven had to forcibly put them to the back of her mind, for a car was flung towards her. She ran out of its path.

"Walker, Kindle, Lynk, be careful."

"You be careful as well, Raven, this isn't an ordinary wind."

"You got that right; it's turned into a ferocious hurricane."

Raven followed Kindle's lead, keeping close as he rode the wind. She watched in amazement when he swiftly evaded anything that flew towards him. As Raven, Walker and Lynk followed Kindle, all found they were learning to manage the wind.

"Kindle, make sure you stay in close proximity but ride the wind."

"You got it, Raven."

Raven struggled to keep her balance, as the force of the wind threatened to lift her up. As she struggled, she noticed a silhouette in the far distance.

"What's that silhouette in the distance?"

Curious about the silhouette, Raven plucked up her courage and battled on through the vicious wind. Suddenly, several branches shot forwards, she evaded some of them, but one hit her in the side and knocked her down.

Hurt from the blow to the side, Raven stood upright again. Grimacing, she screamed in anger at the breeze "Calm down, Breeze, ease off!" keeping her scythe in hand, just in case. To her amazement, the wind seemed a little calmer; she vainly thought her emotional outburst made it calmer than before.

"The wind can't possibly be calming down because I shouted the command, no, no, it couldn't be possible." But nevertheless, Raven had a sneaky pleasure that it seemed that the wind calmed to her command.

Luckily for her, Kindle's eyesight was better than hers, he could help her spot danger. However, nobody saw anything coming, until Raven ducked. An oil tanker crashed, like a jet aircraft and landed on its side with a deafening thud. She went to examine the tanker, and as she examined it, Raven noticed a few drops of oil; worried this would get worse she asked Kindle, Walker and Lynk how to stem this flow. Otherwise, it would leak into the gutters and reach the streams and rivers cause an environmental disaster, it would destroy wildlife and fish and cause massive pollution and contaminate the water supply for people. So, she covered the area with soil to stem any drips and wedged a container underneath, she peered into the cab to see if there were any survivors, the driver seemed shocked but unharmed and he promptly alerted the emergency services, this would mean that people could salvage the situation when the hurricane subsided and prevent further damage to both animals and humans alike.

"Kindle, look out."

"The same for you, Raven."

But their voices were drowned out in the commotion.

A look of panic crossed her face, and she looked anxiously for Kindle, her heart thumping.

Suddenly, Raven heard a loud screech followed by beating wings. She looked up fearfully, her heart constricted with dread, a lump formed in her throat. Upon looking up, relief washed over her, Kindle was flying above.

"Kindle, please don't do that again, you scared me!"

"Raven, I'm supposed to be watching out for danger, so I go far ahead, would you rather you didn't know what's coming and I was just trying to let you know that I'm around."

"I guess you make a good point, I still can't help worrying about you, though."

Kindle looked at Raven; his deep golden eyes were full of concern.

"I know you care about me, Raven, but I need to ensure the path ahead is safe."

"I see but, try and stay a little close."

"I'll try; I'll need to be in front though."

After that little talk with Raven, Kindle resumed his position ahead of her, taking care to stay reasonably close. Suddenly, another vicious wind gust came, Raven ducked while Kindle rode it.

Raven found that she was almost being thrown to the floor. The wind yanked at her like an unruly dog, determined to pull its master over.

Suddenly, a rusty old pylon shot towards Raven. She raised her scythe readily, slicing it diagonally like a knife through bread. The pylon broke in two, as it landed on the floor on either side of her.

"Nice move, Raven."

"Kindle, do you see anything yet?"

"No, but you still have to stay vigilant."

"Thanks for the heads up, Kindle, but we should try and keep an eye out for that figure."

"Good idea, we'll see whether its friend or foe."

"Although I couldn't really see, it appeared to be chained."

"You could be right, Raven, but you still can't make assumptions."

"How am I making assumptions?"

"By stating something that might not even be true."

"Honestly, the pair of you, you're arguing like two spoilt five-year-olds over something that you don't know about."

"But, Walker, I know about it because I saw its silhouette in the distance."

"Whereabouts?"

"It'll become more visible as it gets lighter."

As Raven, Walker and Lynk trailed Kindle; the silhouette was getting bigger and more noticeable. However, what Raven had to be prepared for, wasn't the silhouette but the dangers in the hurricane.

A small plane shot through the wind. Raven promptly readied her scythe, she swung it diagonally, its blade glowed light blue, engaging its magnetic element and slowly steadying the plane and helping it land safely, the pilot staggered out of the cockpit, amazed "Phew, I was certain I was going to crash, I can't understand how I landed safely, something saved my life." She felt relieved and satisfied that she had made a difference. With a spring in her step, Raven refocused her mind on the ever-growing silhouette.

"Are we any closer to finding out what it is?"

"With each step, it'll become clearer."

Curiously, Raven moved towards the blur.

Finally, it seemed the ever-ferocious wind seemed to be tiring from its tirade! She and the others moved through it with ease now.

She began to mentally analyze the blurry figure. She could see four furry legs and a powerful body, which seemed to be covered with thick black fur.

Though Raven's fear was strong, she studied its pointed ears and long broad snout. She also took note of its cold, hard blue eyes. She was standing face to face with a wolf!

However, despite her fear of the wolf, she noticed he was chained. She felt sorry for him, and her soft nature wanted to release him, but could she *trust* him. What if he harmed her? She needed to safeguard herself. She looked at him carefully and despite her concerns, felt affection for him, she liked animals anyway-but thought wolves were really enigmatic. She felt a desire to release him.

"This is a predator, Raven."

"I know that, Kindle."

Raven felt as if she understood him. Some people speak and one believes them, only to discover they are lying years later. But silence has a language of its own, which is immensely powerful; but nobody stops to listen to it as we are all attuned to noise, to speech. The louder it is, the more we are shocked into listening. But in all that loudness people forget the language of silence, of thoughts transmitting to each other quietly. The wolf's unspoken words; his thoughts were being transmitted and understood by Raven. She could feel his vibration, it was pleading harmless and lonely. She decided in that instant to ignore his baring of teeth and snarling but to pay attention to what she was sensing about him. Yes, she was drawn to him and wanted to give him a chance. Kindle, Walker and Lynk were more cautious and warned her. But she felt her sixth senses had served her well in this journey, so she readied her scythe, but this time, she aimed at the chains and shackles. A stream of lightning shot from the blade, shattering them.

Now free, the wolf stood up, baring his huge teeth, before trotting forward. The lightning had spooked him. Still nervous of its imposing look, Raven took a step back.

"What's your name and why were you chained?" she asked gently.

"My name is Phantom, and I was chained for my livestock consumption, I can see that you have freed me and for that I am grateful."

"We need to eat to live but, Phantom-if you like you can come with us, but with your new freedom you're free to choose your own path. If you decide to come with us our path is uncertain, hazardous and we traverse across realms and time zones. There is never a guarantee where we might find ourselves. It could be the past, the present or even the future."

Phantom hesitated and silently took his position in between Raven, Walker and Lynk; his eyes glinting with pure intentions of new friendship. However, Raven still wondered if her senses about the wolf were telling the truth.

The wind had thrust a train car in front of them. Raven instinctively entered with all her companions. No sooner had they taken a seat, it hurtled into the unknown.

Every exit was an end and a beginning so there was always relief, excitement, and hope; it was a strange mixture of emotions. She was getting stronger, braver, and more confident after all her recent experiences. She was learning from everything she went through. Her glance stopped at Phantom and she learned that kindness could yield more rewards than she could have ever imagined, in this case, the friendship of a wolf.

Amber searched high and low; she set out with Taz and Sajid on a windy day and Taz sniffed an abandoned kite that looked like the one Raven flew in the past, it also had Raven's name on it. They took the kite and examined it. Perhaps it was a sign.

John Rahway

Chapter Fifteen

Avoiding Paralysis

Raven found herself, with her companions in front of an open door leading into an imposing stately home. Pivoting round, she took in the vista of the rolling fields all around. The sun was at its zenith and warming the crops all around. The day was hot, a scorcher. Raven tapped into her intuition to ascertain what was required of her. Her gut feeling indicated that her task was indoors so she moved towards the beckoning open door. Her companions stepped in with her. Shockingly, it was a huge contrast from the gloriously sunny outdoors to the gloom and darkness indoors. She regretted coming in and her skin rose up in Goosebumps in the dark, she saw that the huge ornate mirrors were covered in white cloth. The paintings though hard to decipher in the gloom seemed dust laden. The windows had thick curtains barring all light from entering, she was glad of the little light from the open door. She whispered to her companions, "This is very unusual for the house to be so dark. But I'm glad of the door being ajar." But as soon as she said this the heavy door creaked shut! It became spookily dark with the door shut. It seemed like there was nobody home but why did her instinct clearly guide her in as if she was being awaited with great urgency. Although she couldn't see anyone, she could definitely feel a presence. As her eyes adjusted to the gloom, she could make out doors in the hallway. She opened one, it was empty. So, she proceeded to try the next one and found herself in a large room, resembling a dormitory. Lynk, Walker's Alaskan malamute could immediately sense distress and growled.

"What's up, Lynk?"

"Lynk has picked up the negative energy here."

Raven could make out rows of beds throughout, like a hospital with patients of all ages "Help me!" a teenage lad called "We have all been disabled by the ghost of Shabbington Manor". She could see a family confined to their beds barely alive, unable to move; living a miserable existence. A strange realization came over Raven, that no matter how rich, beautiful or opulent a place was, peace and happiness came from good health, peoples' kind behavior and willingness to help each other. "*Harmonious relations could make even a tiny home a pleasant abode.*" Raven thought. She noticed that there was everything money could buy in this house, yet lots of suffering.

Raven inquired further as to what had happened. The sight of the paralyzed people in beds shocked her. She searched her mind to see how she could help them. Raven listened to the young lad who explained about the ghost who could use his gaze to paralyze whoever he chose.

"This is how we have become paralyzed, if you could help us there is some antidote which can reverse the paralysis, but I don't know where it's kept. Everyone else here is resigned to their fate but I am still hopeful that we can recover. Can you help us?"

"I shall try." She knew she needed to keep her wits about her, because she didn't want to end up like them! "*Poor things somehow ended up almost dead.*" She wondered how to reverse this. Her thoughts raced through her mind, how she could avoid the same fate, when she didn't know who the enemy was. She couldn't leave them. But, if she didn't look after herself and her own safety, then she might end up paralyzed. She needed to remain vigilant. Her conscience troubled her. But, was this a trap?

Suddenly, a ghost with long arms that ended in clawed hands and eight long tentacles appeared. Raven took in its frightful form.

"So, I have to fight you?"

"No, not quite, but you'll have to battle against paralysis."

"What?"

"You will have to battle against being paralyzed and you have two hours, in which you must avoid my stare, for if you come into contact with my stare, you'll be paralyzed."

Raven avoided looking at the ghost.

"The paralysis is only breakable by drinking a drop of the antidote, if my stare touches you, you'll be paralyzed for five minutes and the challenge starts as soon as I fly into the shadows, the antidote is to the left of you and you're trespassing, invading my privacy, learning the secrets of my home and you must pay."

Raven turned her eyes to the left, and noticed a small wooden table; with a bottle of dark blue liquid and a syringe. An hourglass full of sand started to release its contents.

"The time starts now."

Raven swiftly swiped the liquid.

The ghost disappeared into the shadows, Raven moved stealthily to the left, remaining watchful. The sand flowed.

"So far so good, as long as I keep the right distance from the ghost, I'll be ok."

"Raven, I wouldn't get overconfident, the ghost can fly." Walker warned her.

"Kindle can fly round him."

"But be careful of the gaze."

"I'll distract him."

"Let's keep out of the dark."

"Excellent plan."

Unfortunately, the ghost had overheard, it flew from the right, its shadow ominous. Raven barely had a chance to react, she narrowly ducked down. The ghost's eyes glowed and green laser beams shot out of them.

Something flew through the ghost, Raven looked up and saw Kindle's pecks going through it, to his shock!

"That's it, Kindle, and keep the ghost off." Raven barked.

"I can't hold him off indefinitely, but I can keep him at bay for now." Kindle assured.

"Be careful of those eye lasers, in other words avoid his face," Raven instructed. "Walker, take your angel form, so you can't be seen to be shot at."

Immediately reverting to his angel form, Walker disappeared from plain sight.

Raven, Lynk and Phantom tried to hide in the darkness, only edging out while the ghost was distracted. Raven had a thought that perhaps his lasers were only effective in the dark.

"Walker, you, Lynk and Phantom, start undoing the curtains, letting the light in and pull all the drapes off of the mirrors!" Raven yelled "I think his weakness is the light!"

The green lasers shot out of its eyes, this time striking Raven, paralyzing her. However, just before she was hit, she managed to call out to Walker.

"Walker, if I get paralyzed, use the antidote to get me back."

"Sure thing, Raven." Walker responded.

Walker, with the loaded syringe in hand, evaded the ghost's laser, with his invisibility in angel form, quickly administered the antidote. She quickly returned to normal.

But then, Phantom looked up, his gaze accidentally met the lasers.

"Move, now!" too late

Quick as lightning, Raven moved into the bright light created by removing the drapes, her heart thumped violently but she noticed the lasers were much weaker in the light. However, she saw Phantom fall in a catatonic state; she rushed to get the antidote to him.

Phantom howled and regained his freedom, and shrunk away from the ghost, Raven glanced at the sand timer, and felt she needed to rush and get the antidote to the paralyzed people before time ran out.

The falling sand heightened her fear and sense of urgency of not getting the antidote to them in time. Conversely, self-preservation made her feel relieved that the sand was signaling the end of the ordeal.

"Kindle; make sure you keep him at bay." Raven ordered.

Raven deftly kept opening curtains and windows to keep the shadows out, weaken his power and restore hope to the household. She took the opportunity to put a few drops of the antidote into a paralyzed young patient. He looked approximately her age, seemed young and strong and she felt if she could unlock him, he would be of great use administering the antidote to others. She wasn't sure if it would work, but it was worth a try. She took a few drops and smeared them inside his mouth, on his tongue, his gums and all around his mouth. It absorbed into his body quite quickly, and she saw that he started to move. She roughly massaged his hands and arms, feet and lower legs to get his circulation moving.

"Thank you, I'm Jay."

"Jay, go around, and put this in everybody's mouths as soon as you can?" Ravens ordered "and rub their limbs to get them moving, Phantom, you and Lynk grab as many hand mirror shields as you can to use against the ghost's lasers."

Raven looked fretfully over her shoulder; the ghost was advancing, using his many arms to close the drapes they had opened, and deepening the gloom in the house.

"So, you still want to paralyze me?"

"Of course, I do."

"Well, I hate to break this terrible news to you; you don't have much time for that because if you looked at the sand timer, then you'd notice the amount of sand left."

The ghost looked up at the sand timer, there was much less sand at the top than the bottom, a vicious look crossed his face and he would fight even harder.

Phantom handed her a mirror. Whilst ducking she was able to deflect his lasers back to him. He yelped in realization and his step faltered as his own lasers hit him as they bounced back at him from the mirror she was using as a shield. Visibly weakened and slower the ghost was becoming lethargic.

All of a sudden, everyone in the room was using mirror shields to protect themselves and deflect his lasers back at him. Hit multiple times, he crashed to the floor paralyzed.

"Quick, everyone, reopen all the curtains he closed." Barked Raven. "Open windows and doors."

Light streamed in. Defeated, the dark disappeared. Life giving air breezed in. The ghost was vaporizing in front of their eyes. Finishing the fear.

Finally free, the people of the house approached Raven to thank her for freeing them from the prison of their own bodies, standing upright, Jay's parents said "we don't know how long we would have been stuck in that catatonic state if it hadn't been for you all. Thank you seems so inadequate a word, for our gratitude and appreciation is immense."

Raven noticed that the somber silence of the house, turned into joyful squeals as the children ran about chasing one another. The normal hustle and bustle of the house returned. Wonderfully tempting and tantalizing aromas arose from the kitchen.

Raven reflected as to how desperate she was to leave here. Now, with the warmth and welcoming environment, she wished to stay and be part of this family. But knew nevertheless that soon enough, she would outstay her welcome because this wasn't really her family.

She would have to move on in her quest to defeat Mephistopheles and save the precious gems from his clutches, and prevent him from inciting humans to destroy each other.

Raven stayed for a while, she and her companions ate and drank, played with the children and relaxed and got to know one another. The children played with Phantom and Lynk frolicking in the sunshine. Not desiring to leave, she had got better at working out the different modes of exit and she suspected to leave this realm, she would have to walk beyond the fields.

Along with her companions, Raven then reluctantly took leave and they walked through the fields. They became a spec before disappearing from sight altogether.

Amber was glad on having found the kite, she had Taz sniff it and when he did he barked, recognizing Raven's scent from it.

"Raven's definitely alive somewhere." Amber smiled. "I'll find her soon enough."

Dark Rise: The Nightmares' Isolation

Chapter Sixteen

Everlasting Famine

R aven took in the sight of long expanses of land that stretched far into the horizon. Empty and eerily quiet. The land looked parched, the trees dusty, and the heat intensifying. For a while, it felt good to have some light and warmth after being in the darkened room with paralyzed people and the ghost, but it was getting unbearably hot. The sun was beating down. She began to notice there was hardly any greenery; the land, arid brown into the horizon.

The companions rested, assessed their surroundings deciding to explore this new realm. The silence, peaceful at first became deafening. They noticed the heat had destroyed the crops. Worse still, they saw a number of dead livestock lying on the malnourished earth. Raven, crestfallen to see this had hoped to get through this realm as peacefully as possible. Forcing herself to focus, she suddenly wanted to convince people to care for those in difficult situations, to make sure everyone had access to clean, fresh drinking water to irrigate crops, feed livestock and have a healthy life. It was unjust that some had everything and were wasteful, consuming most of the earth's resources and throwing much away. Then, there were parts of the world where people had no food or water. Not fair! She saw muddy dried-up streams, filled with animal faeces and insect larvae; desperate children were drinking this! She wanted to end the suffering.

"Kindle; is this the only drinking water that you can see that people have access to?"

"I'm afraid so, Raven, this looks like the only water source for miles, a festering bed of disease."

With a troubled heart, she explored down the hard, cracked mud path, looking for someone to explain this.

"It seems awfully quiet."

"Raven, stay vigilant."

"This silence is scary."

"I don't like people knowing my fears, especially not Mephistopheles."

She felt this lifeless environment, harbored sinister secrets. She needed, for her sanity, to find small nuggets of good in the surroundings she repeatedly found herself in or she would not stay emotionally and mentally strong. Walker, being an angel knight could sense Raven's disquiet, so helpfully suggested that she list everything that had gone well to calm her frightening mental conversations with herself. Taking his advice, she started to make a list of things to be thankful about.

"I am fit and well, I am intelligent and have succeeded in outwitting a dragon to enter The Nightmare Rift, I was able to control my emotions when witnessing the sharks eating shipwreck victims, I administered medicine to all the injured people with speed and agility. From being alone, I seem to have gathered loyal and diverse friends who have accompanied me through good and difficult times." Though she couldn't remember her distant past, she realized that she could remember recent events since leaving the hostel but anything before the hostel, sadly eluded her.

The animal carcasses told the fact that food and water was scarce. She wondered if humans had died too! Raven wondered if they had died from famine, she knew it was always animals that suffered and were neglected first in times of scarcity. But there were signs of conflict as some animals also had bullet wounds. She wondered if one of the causes of famine had been conflict where people were restricting each other's water supply and damaging crops. *"Why oh why can't people compromise instead of having conflict."* As people strived to stay alive their animals were the first casualty. The very animals they had depended on for working their land, for milk, eggs, meat, riding and companionship.

"Their precious and faithful animals had given up the struggle and died."

Although her past was a mystery to her, there were certain things she knew instinctively but couldn't remember where or how she had learnt them. She recalled that some traditions and narrations of old, Judaism, Christianity, and Islam all had stories in their books, Torah, Bible and Quran of a man called Noah. Noah at the time of the flood was inspired to save animals two of each. She smiled ruefully to herself; that if men today were drowning; they would never bother to take the animals on their boat. They would just reserve it for people who could pay, or they would be too afraid of sinking or being devoured by lions, tigers, snakes, or wolves.

"Humans are greedy and selfish on many levels." Thought Raven. But she consoled herself with the next thought that many were brave and compassionate and cared deeply to help.

But nevertheless, nature had been destroyed, trees felled to make way for concrete buildings and roads, causing climate change, affecting rainfall, causing flooding in some areas, drought, food shortage and famine in others. Whilst the windmills didn't turn or move, animals died from lack of rain and food, amongst the dying crops.

No one was visible, yet she felt a sense of foreboding, a premonition of a presence.

Ears pricked, senses alert, she heard a deep, malicious voice that sent an icy cold shiver down her spine.

"HEAR ME, CLOUDS, REMAIN FULL DO NOT EMPTY YOUR CONTENTS!"

"Did you hear that?" asked Raven

"I did but I can't see anything." Walker told her.

"I can't see anything either, but we should try and get out of here quick." Phantom added.

"That's a good idea, Phantom.

Suddenly, her blood turned to ice as the voice sounded closer.

"So long as my magic seals the clouds, this famine shall be eternal."

"It's that voice again!" Raven breathed "Kindle, can you fly and see who it is."

Kindle flew ahead; eyes fixed on the distance.

A loud whinnying rang out, startling Raven.

"What was that?" Raven asked anxiously.

"A horse!"

Kindle had seen something and urgently returned to share the news. His gold eyes concerned.

"Kindle, what did you find out?" probed Raven.

"I could make out a powerful rider on a horse with glowing red eyes."

"I should've known there's something sinister here."

"Don't panic, Raven; let's not assume the worst." Walker placated her.

The whinnying boomed nearer, much louder and more frightening.

Raven tensed, her recent past experiences in The Nightmare Rift had scared her but also increased her resilience.

"That sounds like a very strong and intimidating animal? But how would anything survive this famine? Unless?" Raven asked herself.

"Raven, don't start freaking out, I'm sure it isn't what you think it is." Walker tried to assure her.

"I've got a bad feeling about this." Said Raven in a trembling voice.

When the whinnying sounded again, Raven looked frantically for somewhere to hide. All she found was a clump of dying bushes, although they didn't look big enough to hide behind, she tried anyway.

Partially hidden, she spotted a creature with spiked hooves, silhouetted in the distance. She decided to re-emerge, hiding the fear deep within.

"Why did you hide just then, Raven?" asked Kindle.

"To buy time."

Raven put on a brave face and walked towards the silhouette. She could see the eyes; their imposing glare made her blood turn to ice, but deliberately ignoring the dread that had quietly snuck into her heart, like a fox sneaking into a farm at night, she boldly marched forward.

"This famine has killed pretty much everything; how can this horse survive?"

"We'll have to find out."

She beheld, a huge black horse; and he who sat on it had a pair of scales in his hand. The scales were the giveaway; she was facing Famine, the third horseman of the Apocalypse. The huge horse whinnied with fury, before rearing up on its hind legs. Raven stared Famine down, with a fake mask of confidence concealing her rising fear. She realized that the horseman had a great advantage over her, but she needed to stop the famine. She introduced herself

"I'm Raven."

"Famine." Said the horseman.

"You look well while everyone is suffering." Raven felt a tinge of anger.

"I could say the same for you."

"Do you know what has caused this devastation?"

"When people are engaged in fighting and hurting each other for greed then the end result is normally famine." Famine explained.

"Would you help me put an end to this and help reinstate their water supply so they can feed themselves and their animals?"

"That's a very noble cause, young lady, and you look like you're on a mission." Said Famine, eyeing her scythe and healing water. "If you can defeat me, famine shall vaporize and leave."

"Let the duel begin."

She silently petitioned Zirnitra her Slavic dragon god, she had faith in.

"I'm at a great disadvantage against Famine. His horse can trample and hurt me with its spiked hooves, help me find a way of battling him in a way we are both evenly matched."

"Raven, I know well that you will struggle if you battle Famine on foot, for he has a much greater advantage over you, so to help you, I have sent you a steed who is most valiant and strong."

She heard and visualized the powerful black dragon with bat like wings and glowing purple eyes. She didn't care if Zirnitra was real or not but imagining this made her feel strong.

Raven looked to her right, where to her surprise she saw a great and muscular fully equipped red-brown stallion walking towards her.

The steed Altair whinnied and reared as Raven mounted him, ready to battle. Raven gently nudged him in the sides and raised her scythe, Altair galloped in Famine's direction.

The scales disappeared. Famine extracted his halberd in their stead.

Famine and Raven charged forwards on their horses; their weapons collided at the midpoint. Both were pushing the other back. Sickening thuds rang out as Raven and Altair hit the ground.

Raven remounted Altair, this time she pointed her scythe at Famine, and a stream of purple lightning shot out. Famine, prompt to retaliate, aimed his halberd and crimson lightning shot towards Raven. The two attacks collided in a stalemate, cancelling each other out.

Famine charged forwards, his halberd pointed at Raven, ready to kill. Raven met him readily; there was a nasty clang as their weapons collided. A loud thud rang as Famine collapsed on the ground; his horse fell on top of him.

While Famine was down, Raven quickly took advantage, aimed her scythe and lightning shot from the blade, shocking him. Electrified, Famine raised his halberd, the crimson lightning shot out. Altair whinnied in pain from the blow.

Famine, to Raven's horror rose back up, his horse whinnied triumphantly. Raven raised her scythe, charged forwards before swinging it. A loud clang sounded as Raven's scythe collided with Famine's halberd, the weapons locked together.

Raven and Famine pushed their weapons against each other. Both forced with all their strength. Lynk, Walker's invisible angel dog watched the duel, enraged by the mismatch of strength as Raven was falling. He lost control, bared his teeth and let out his ice breath at Famine. Famine staggered from the unexpected blast. Raven hit the floor. Altair also fell hard.

Undeterred Famine capitalized, aiming his halberd at Altair, but the invisible dog struck him again with a blast of ice, buying Raven some time. Raven aimed her scythe and purple thunder rang out. The scythe's electricity collided with Famine's lightning, Famine looked at his halberd, the purple bolts had knocked the blade off. As he used his scales to repair it, Raven quickly took the opportunity to give the healing water to Altair.

"Is he doing what I think he's doing?" Raven said irritably.

"Yes, unfortunately for you he is." Walker replied. "Raven, I can help you if you want."

"I can use all the help I can get."

Famine, with his halberd repaired, aimed at Raven, the crimson lightning flowed forwards, Raven saw it, she retaliated to block it and aimed her scythe. Crackling purple bolts shot out with the collision. A clamorous explosion sent dust flying everywhere, as the two attacks repelled each other.

The smoke cleared, Raven prepared to strike. However, Famine realized and charged forwards. As the halberd came down, Raven swung her scythe; a tumultuous bang shook the environment.

Both horses were shaken from the bang. Altair was hobbling. Famine, upon seeing this, pointed his halberd at both Raven and Altair. At this point both Walker and Lynk shot forwards to spook Famine's horse, whilst Kindle swooped past Famine's face and knocked him from his mount. Raven valiantly raised her scythe and shot at Famine, but the horseman leapt aside.

Famine swung his halberd straight towards her. The blade just inches from her throat, she summoned enough strength to grab the handle, pushing it back as far as possible. Unable to watch Kindle swooped at Famine's eyes.

Raven gave Altair a light nudge, he charged forwards with blazing eyes. Famine aimed his halberd; its blade at her chest. Kindle returned to swoop as Lynk also unleashed his ice breath at Famine, buying precious time.

Raven and Famine fought bitterly. Neither wanted to give up. Famine fell from his horse, Raven, quick to take advantage, jarred him with a bolt of purple lightning.

A surge of horror slammed Raven when she saw Famine gradually rising up.

"You're recovering so quickly." said Raven.

"I'm afraid so, you little fool."

Famine rose through the electrical blast, mounted his horse again, his halberd ready and pointed at Raven. Her eyes narrowed, she aimed her scythe at him, the purple bolt shot out again. Famine pre-empted the move, the crimson lightning flowed out and the attacks hit a stalemate.

Famine had come off worse, for when he looked at his hand, he saw his fingers had been shocked off.

Raven quickly swung her scythe, the blade shot downwards. Famine was prompt to respond, and a deafening bang flooded the area. With all her strength, Raven pushed forwards as hard as she could, tiredness was weighing down on her.

Famine, not one to give in easily, pushed back just as hard, the two blades were locked together. Famine vigorously and forcefully carried on pushing. Raven barely hung on, her fingers were gripping both her scythe and the reigns.

"I'm not going to let you win."

Famine fell to the ground. Her enemy grounded, Raven struck again, she slammed her scythe onto Famine's arm.

Famine's arm shattered; Raven raised her scythe again, ready to finish him off. However, before she could act, Famine's arm regenerated and he used his halberd to block her.

"No way, how did you do that?"

Disbelief flooded Raven, and she watched fretfully as Famine remounted his horse. Raven heard a clang, and noticed Altair's broken chest armor lying on the floor.

"Oh, did I forget to tell you that my lightning could break metal?"

"No, but I'll see that you fall the same."

Altair charged towards Famine, but without his armor his chest was sliced open. Raven tended to him with tears burning in her eyes. Quick as lightning, Raven knelt and extracted her water, pouring it on the deep, hideous wound, while stroking his neck, trying to comfort the exhausted horse.

"It's too late."

"Altair, please don't say that." Said Raven sadly. "We still have to fight Famine."

"I expect you to bring him down, give it everything you have."

Having encouraged Raven, Altair's eyes rolled up in his head which fell limply, and he was asleep. Raven rose to her feet, allowing the tears to fall without wiping them off.

"How sentimental, little girl." Famine commented "What a tearful mess you are."

Ignoring Famine's comment, she defiantly aimed her scythe at him, catching him off guard, making him fall with a thud.

"Pride before a fall!"

Maddened, dirt flew into the air as Famine charged forward. Raven stood still. She raised her scythe, the blade pointing forward; she observed the horse's movement.

Famine's blade missed Raven. Now, both Raven and Famine would fight on foot, to determine it all.

Famine stood at full height, but to Raven's surprise he kept his scale out. Adrenaline stopped her from being dismayed, she had to act.

"Now, Raven!" She heard Walker shout, she raised her scythe and the purple electricity zigzagged towards Famine. However, much to Raven's dismay, the lightning bounced off Famine.

"What the heck?"

"I hate to tell you this, but Famine's scale is glowing and it's creating a barrier round him."

"Any ideas, Walker?" asked Raven.

Raven, launch a continuous attack at the scale?" Walker suggested.

She launched a volley of electric bolts at the barrier and scale.

The barrier disintegrated and the lightning shattered Famine's scale to pieces.

"It's over, Famine."

"I still have life left and I'm going to destroy you."

"You're welcome to try."

Famine swung his halberd, the blade aimed towards Raven, she ferociously slashed back. Each trying to overwhelm the other.

With one final push, Famine toppled. She aimed her scythe, ready to wrap it up. The crackling electricity shocked Famine, he screamed in pain as the velocity increased.

Famine and his horse vaporized, disappearing into thin air. His chest split open, a ball of light emerged, becoming black smoke. This suddenly transformed into a feather, the palest of white, ominous glow surrounding it.

"Let's move, that feather's harmful" Raven yelled.

They ran from where Famine once stood. The feather flew up, let out a blast, shocking the clouds that Famine had sealed to release replenishing rain.

Suddenly, there were puddles with raindrops dancing amidst the sunshine! A huge colorful rainbow appeared in celebration. Raven spread out her arms and lifted her head up to the rain, soaking up the cleansing drops, enjoying the freshness, the coolness on her skin. She felt triumphant. Altair, feeling the raindrops splattering all over him woke up and trotted over for a celebratory nuzzle. Laughing heartily, she put her arms round him in a huge hug.

The wolf, the Malamute, Walker and Kindle gathered round.

"Thanks for keeping your word, Famine!" yelled Raven, as the rainbow beckoned them towards its colours.

Amber crossed off more locations on the map; each one fuelled her determination to find Raven. Taz returned with a kite he refused to leave; Amber took it from him and found the letter R in one corner. Her heart leapt.

John Rahway

Dark Rise: The Nightmares' Isolation

Chapter Seventeen

Mistaken Judgment

*D*awn arrived in a snowcapped mountainous area. It looked like someone had a lot of pleasure painting it. The rolling lands looked beautiful, well loved by its artist. The winter sun hung above like a beacon of hope, a guide for lost travelers. Raven consciously decided to soak up the scenery and live just in this picturesque moment, even just for a short while to just breathe and be. She had realized, one had to pause to enjoy time and replenish oneself because nobody ever knew what was round the corner.

Raven's fingers were chilled from the biting wind that piled up the soft beautiful snow, falling gently like summer's rain. Of course, this was freezing cold snow that could be made into snowballs. Many snowflakes found unlikely homes in Raven's long flowing black hair and her cloak. Although she was shivering and the wind was making her eyes water, she knelt and made a snowball, which she playfully tossed at Walker.

"Raven, are you sure you want to play snowballs?"

A mischievous smile crossed Raven's face; she picked up a ball of snow in her gloveless hands and threw it. The snowball hit Walker in the arm. Unlike Raven, Walker was an angel knight, so he felt no pain. He picked up a snowball and tossed it, Raven giggled as she took the hit before returning fire.

Smiling widely, Raven made another snowball, and tossed it. It found Walker's shoulder before falling off. Although this snow-clad environment could well be another nightmare, Raven felt thankful that she could at least find pleasure in it. She was intent on enjoying her journey wherever she possibly could, so she laughed heartily, giggled, and squealed with delight, enjoying the company of her companions. Such joy was contagious and soon everyone was laughing and having fun together, Lynk and Phantom caught in the crossfire, yelped and ran away. No one realized how much time had elapsed. But then the snow started slipping down the mountain, gathering ever-growing momentum. Kindle soared above the vista whilst they played and noticed the snow cracking, hurtling down the mountain.

"Raven, we've got trouble." warned Kindle.

"What kind of trouble, Kindle?"

There was a thunderous noise, and Raven saw the snow shooting down. She turned and ran, but it was fruitless. The avalanche shot down over her like a jet plane.

Ensnared under the avalanche, Raven could only hope and pray that someone would save her. She screamed out to her unknown family in her mind "Save me!!" Cold and scared, Raven allowed her eyes to water and the tears to freeze. With her bare hands, she attempted to dig her way out of this icy grave. It felt impossible, the heaviness of the snow weighing her down.

Buried under the avalanche, Raven could hear a loud pounding of paws.

"I hope that's help." Thought Raven.

Hopeful and fearful, she hoped that she would be freed quickly. Petrified, she wouldn't be dug out in time, that she would die waiting, she tried to find a pocket of air.

Raven could hear scrabbling of paws, the shifting of snow. Relief washed over her. Three pairs of paws became visible; she instantly recognized the black paws, the panting breath then Phantom's wolfish head. The second pair of white paws was Lynk's. However, the white paws and brown and white head with the floppy ears and droopy jowls belonged to a large Saint Bernard with a thick coat and warm brown eyes.

Phantom, Lynk and the Saint Bernard dug until Raven was visible. She was pleased to see them. Shivering from fear and cold, she reached for the huge dog's keg, though she could barely hold it, she uncorked it and gratefully drank the warming drink to give her the warmth she craved so badly.

"Thank you for helping me, I'm Raven"

"My name is Titan and I rescue people who are trapped in avalanches."

"I'm very grateful to all of you"

Titan led them to a cave in the snow, Walker helped start a fire. They all sat around chatting and thawing out together.

Titan talked about his life rescuing people in avalanches. Raven asked if there was anything she could do to repay the favor.

"Well," said Titan hesitantly "If you can aid me in taking down Wizeador, the ice dragon king, he killed my elder brother Atlas. I would also like him to restore spring to stop the danger from avalanches to passing travelers. I am getting old and tired, and I cannot continue to rescue people for much longer."

Raven was incensed by what Titan had told her about how Atlas was killed, she was grateful to him for saving her, so she believed him without verifying or checking it through. She was so thankful; she immediately wanted to help him in return. She marched with all fervor to find and confront the dragon.

"I'll try my best, Titan."

Grateful for being saved, Raven stroked Phantom, Lynk and Titan before she followed them to meet Kindle and Walker.

"Walker, Kindle, we have a new directive, in that we have to attempt to persuade the ice dragon Wizeador to restore spring."

"Let's go then."

Raven took a sip of her healing water; it cleansed her and healed the cold.

Flying above a dark mountain, Kindle could see a cave mouth of impenetrable blackness.

"What's that cave?"

"It must be home to a creature."

After an exhausting walk, Raven and her friends made it to the mouth of the cave. She entered slowly and cautiously, the cave was huge and spacious and perennial ice lined all sides, while Raven trod carefully to try and avoid slipping on any black ice. Freezing cold air flowed through the glacier cave, but that was the least of Raven's worries because who knew what creature could be there or whether they would be friendly. Before long, Raven reached the cave's heart and a huge ice dragon with dark teal scales, icy horns and claws, narrow yellow eyes and enormous bat like wings, tipped with ice, flew from the darkness, settling on the frozen ground in front of Raven, he roared with fury, his huge teeth just inches away from Raven.

Upon seeing Raven, the dragon looked her over with a quizzical gaze but Raven was full of fury, and thought he was a vengeful creature.

"I am Wizeador Dragon King of the Frigid Land, who are you and why have you come here and disturbed my rest?"

Raven respectfully curtseyed in front of the great dragon before introducing herself.

"I'm Raven, and I have only come to ask that you allow spring to return, Your Majesty."

"I will not allow such an atrocity to happen in my kingdom."

"Either you restore spring, or you will die."

The dragon was furious at this rudeness, he could have used his powerful icy breath to kill Raven where she stood, but he didn't. Luckily for Raven, Wizeador was a wise dragon who was apparently well meaning. He asked a series of questions of Raven.

"Have you had any thoughts of what will happen to the polar bears, the penguins, the walruses, the arctic wolves and the wildlife residing on the ice cap? Have you any consideration for the destruction that will happen when ice melts, the sea levels rise and drown the world?"

Raven was lost for words, and she realized that she had not thought it through and felt a pang of guilt as she was starting to realize that the dragon's argument had logic, some places are meant to be cold to keep the balance.

"Why did you kill Atlas?"

Titan also listened in intently.

"Atlas was a beloved and faithful rescue dog; he saved many a life trapped in the snow and avalanches. There are many people who owe their lives to him. Sadly, he contracted rabies and an agonizing decision had to be made to put him to sleep. He had to regrettably enter the afterlife to save him from suffering further and to prevent others from contracting the disease and suffering as well. Young lady, you must not jump to conclusions without gathering all the facts."

Guilt engulfed Raven as Titan also went quiet, as he too realized that in his grief at the loss of his brother; he had nearly made a huge mistake.

Raven realized she had felt an apology was due; she humbly apologized and sought to build a better relationship and repair any hurt or damage she might have unknowingly caused Wizeador. She felt that she had learned an important lesson that there are two sides to every story, and one must gather all the facts before acting lest a grave mistake be made. She kicked herself inwardly for being so ready to start a fight when a simple discussion, a conversation can clear a problem especially if people are ready to compromise.

Wizeador could see that Raven was genuinely remorseful and had seemed to have learned a salutary lesson, so he melted at Raven's apology and treated her well. He also understood Titan's grief and was glad to lay his misconceptions to rest. Raven vowed never to jump to conclusions without checking all the facts.

"Goodbye, Titan, it was nice to have met you and I daresay you would make a great teacher to other puppies who I hope continue your great work of saving lives in the mountains just as you did mine and I hope one day to come back to see you."

"Thank you, Raven, it was nice to have met you as well and thank you for enabling me to find closure over Atlas's death."

"You're welcome, Titan, he'll be proud watching over you."

Before taking leave of Wizeador in the cable car, she admired the beauty all around as she glanced over the snowcapped hills and valleys. Then, her mind turned to Mephistopheles. She explained to the wise dragon how Mephistopheles was withholding the knowledge of her family but had agreed to reunite her with them in exchange for the six precious gems.

"You must be cautious for Mephistopheles cannot be trusted, he will try everything to get the gems. I know that Phobetor is guarding the emerald in The Nightmare Rift. You must prevent him from getting his hands on them."

As Raven thought about all that had happened, she was proud of the successful decisions she had made on her own. She felt that she was thinking for herself as she was dealing with her mistakes. Normally, she found that Mephistopheles was controlling her, he had the greed for the special gems that he was looking for and he wanted people to fight, to argue, families to split up, he wanted people to be enemies. Divide and rule, that was his motto, because if people split, he can go and get to the lonely sheep and control them. He had been trying to control her for ages and now as she made these decisions for herself and peacefully made sure a fair solution and understanding was reached, she knew he would be angry. She smiled to herself at the thought of him jumping up and down in vexation.

"What a nit."

She was pleased with herself, feeling smug as a bug and she decided she would not be subdued or controlled by him. Meanwhile, as she was thinking, Mephistopheles was tuned to her thoughts, aware of what she had done.

"She's getting out of hand; she thinks that by thinking for herself she's going to succeed; I'm not going to let her. I want those gems, and I've observed her; I've put her through the tests and she, so far looks like the best person for it, she's strong, fearless, fast, and kind and it's her kindness that I'm worried about. Her kindness and justice will make me lose, and I can't have that! I will control her! She's going to be my puppet; she will get me my gems and she will do as I command! I am powerful, I control people's whims! I'm not having it! I'm not having it!" He seethed.

Raven sensed his thoughts in her mind. She couldn't hear him, but she could sense him, so she smiled to herself.

"He must be hopping mad………"

Raven was ecstatic she didn't hurt anybody, hadn't started a fight, had made a friend, and she made peace knowing very well Mephistopheles would be livid. Strangely, it made her feel braver and stronger than if she had.

She also realized that although most people and animals enjoy warmth, some places must remain cold to maintain the equilibrium to safeguard all the cold loving creatures.

After an exhaustive and fruitless search Amber decided to take a break to think. She took Taz and went skiing where she and Raven had gone as children. The place was snow clad and reminded Amber of when she played with Raven in the snow. Raven was perpetually in her thoughts, she felt her close! She felt Raven was screaming for her; she looked around everywhere, convinced Raven was connecting with her.

John Rahway

Dark Rise: The Nightmares' Isolation

Chapter Eighteen

To Save A Life

The cable car came to a stop outside the front courtyard of an old house. Raven exited along with her friends, after a scenic journey above the beautiful white landscape, wondering where her journey had brought her. Looking around she saw a stark contrast to the brilliant white she had left behind. She studied the huge courtyard, beautiful and full of striking flowers and birds chirruping. She looked up at the house; its soulless appearance sent a chill down her spine. She could just sense that her next task lay here.

Despite her rising dread, Raven nervously wandered towards the house, the pretty weeds covering the path. A feeling of desolation seemed to be emanating from the house. Suddenly, something slammed into her face and knocked her out of her reflection.

"Oww, what was that?"

"A flying squirrel."

"I didn't know they could fly."

"Squirrels don't actually fly, Raven, it was gliding."

"It just shocked me, Kindle."

Raven gratefully walked closer to her friends, thinking how everything would have seemed colorless and difficult without them. They approached the cold and uninviting house.

"I wonder why we're drawn to this particular house. I wonder what challenge lies within it."

The wind surrounded Raven's body, gently stroking her from her beautiful long black hair to her feet. Her mind and body were alert and alive as if electric.

She was standing on the front porch, she didn't move, but stared curiously through the windows.

"Walker, do you think we should go in?"

"Well, yes, Raven, I don't see any other way."

Raven shook her head and sighed resignedly; she knocked a few times, then turned the doorknob of the sun-bleached yellow door anticlockwise, wiping the mud off her Converses. She and Walker, the angel knight stepped into a dingy, dark entrance hall. The others on guard.

Raven pulled her cloak tightly, to keep herself warm. An open door emitted a striking orange glow, inviting her closer.

"What's that glow and where's it coming from?"

"I think it's coming from back living room."

Though Raven's head told her not to move, her heart had other ideas and she forced herself to rise above fear. She was compelled towards the beautiful light, like a moth about to be singed by the flame.

In the living room, Raven saw a roaring fire crackling in the inglenook. The fire warmed and relaxed her. She could hear the faint tune of a hymn accompanied by soft footsteps.

She was relieved it was just a young girl. Raven saw that she was a pretty girl, slim with long straight chestnut brown hair but looked very depressed. The girl was roughly about her age, perhaps a little younger. The girl looked puzzled when she saw Raven.

"Hello, my name is Raven."

"My name is Chasma and I'm so glad you've come to visit me; I hope you'll stay a while." Said the girl

"I'm not here to stay, I'm just passing through." Raven responded.

"Please stay a little, I'm very lonely." Chasma pleaded.

Something about the girl tugged at her heartstrings. She was intrigued to know what had made her so sad.

Chasma was playing with a string, teasing a fluffy lilac ragdoll cat who was bouncily batting at the yarn with its paws.

"Do you live alone, Chasma?" asked Raven gently.

"Look at the pictures."

Curiously, Raven looked at the faded paintings on the walls that surrounded them, she saw Chasma in some of them with two other girls, a man and two women.

"Is this your family?"

"Yes, that is my mother, she died, and I still miss her terribly. This is my older sister. This is my father. He remarried but yesterday I got a letter saying that he had been killed in action, I just feel so empty without my parents. This is my stepmother and half-sister; they are both away at present. My half-sister and stepmother have a special mother and daughter bond, I always feel like an outsider looking in. However, I am close with my biological sister, and respect her for all the good she does but she's always working. She's a physician and an apothecary, you see; the only one for miles. Sadly, there are so many people who are sick with life threatening illnesses and some who are having babies. So, I tend to spend a lot of my time alone, despondency and depression can encircle me. Sometimes, I wonder what the point of living is and thoughts of ending it come into my head." Chasma's voice cracked, and her eyes brimmed with tears of pain that flowed gently down her face. Raven didn't comfort her; but remained quiet allowing her time to speak and express her feelings. She felt a spark of pity for Chasma, though she didn't know what to do about it. Eventually Raven decided to share her thoughts too, as an introduction of herself.

"You're really lucky to have a family, I don't know where mine is, and I feel quite lost without them. I look at everyone I pass by and look for any signs of recognition or a feeling that connects us, hoping someone will say that they are overjoyed to find me and take me home. I long for parents that will look at me with love and pride, who will hug me and tell me how much they have missed me. I long for siblings with whom I belong and friends to share good times with, I just keep searching every face I see."

Chasma seemed shocked to hear that Raven was all alone in the world. She felt a pang of guilt, for thinking she was the only one going through a difficult time. She looked at Raven's strange companions; Raven saw her glance and explained that these were the friends that she had made on her lonely journey.

"I am so grateful that I met Walker, Lynk, Kindle and Phantom. Without their support and companionship, I doubt that I would have survived some of the scary times that I've been through."

The two girls confided in each other and were shocked at how quickly time had passed. Raven began to enjoy Chasma's company, and they all ate together and played cards and chatted. Her companions happily relaxed in the room warmed by the fire. This is something that Raven had missed in her life. She confided to Chasma that she was being controlled by Mephistopheles in that he wanted her to find the six gems that represent kindness, love, humility, compassion, trust and diligence in exchange for her past memories.

"But I don't trust him, Chasma." said Raven "he's going to double cross me; he already has control of the seven deadly sins."

"How will you ensure that he doesn't take the gems from you, after you do all the hard work to find them and then not give you your memories in return?"

"What he doesn't realize is that I'm onto him and I'm beginning to understand the game he's playing. As I don't want him to cause mayhem and destruction by causing enmities amongst people, I'm going to have to outsmart him."

Raven enjoyed her very human connection with Chasma, the sharing of confidences and joint problem solving. She wanted Chasma to feel that life was worth living and not feel tempted to give up or live in a lonely desolate way. She wanted her to feel self-reliant and not have to depend on others for kindness. Perhaps she could give it instead! With this brain wave, Raven felt compelled to motivate Chasma.

"Chasma, go with your sister, help her to take care of her patients! It will be of help to her, it will ease her workload, give her company. It will give patients better care and give you time with your sister. You will learn new skills and meet new people, learn about their lives and their problems. Chasma, it will make you feel needed, wanted even, and make new friendships. Try it, Chasma."

Chasma was amazed at the simplicity of the solution, she decided that she would definitely try to be useful and look for as many opportunities as possible to be of service. She made up her mind to go out with her sister and serve the community, and she felt after having spoken to Raven that her mind was completely changed from when she constantly felt sorry for herself. She realized that people were going through far greater challenges. She felt that she had been so self-absorbed that she didn't notice anyone else's problems, just her own. Chasma could see now, by helping others, the solutions to one's own problems were often found too. She couldn't wait for her sister to arrive so she could convince her.

Raven understood why she had been drawn to this house; compelled to enter. The house no longer looked gloomy. She stayed with Chasma to support her new way of life. The next morning, Chasma went with her sister. Raven watched as she went house to house with her sister, comforting people, fetching medicines, mixing poultices, reducing fevers, and welcoming babies into the world. She looked more energetic, and purposeful. She was needed and not needy; she was useful and not useless. She was happy. Chasma regaled them with stories of her day, the people she had met and how she had been able to support them and help them. Raven had enjoyed her stay with Chasma and didn't want to leave but had a quest to fulfill.

Drawn towards a mist into another time, another realm, Raven and her companions waved goodbye.

Amber feared for Raven but felt her alive, unable to share her thoughts with anyone, lest they think her mad. She refused to give up and continued the search.

Dark Rise: The Nightmares' Isolation

Chapter Nineteen

Resting the Deceased

Raven looked at the starlit ink black sky above, she was always amazed at where the mists of time transported them. It seemed to her time was an invisible and invincible force, that no one could capture and yet everyone and everything was a prisoner of time. The sun, the moon and the stars and seasons all were captives of time. Each had a role that they carried out and all had to pass quietly within their appointed time. Life was like that, a beginning, a set of experiences, trials, and tests then the inevitable departure, perhaps on to further adventures. Who knew? Death's shadow would always follow, no matter where one went, Raven reflected. Time didn't care for anyone; it just took whosoever at their appointed time. Raven decided to eek the best out of time and live carefree and happy on her journey; wherever that led, rather than just **wait** for good times! She resolved to make the most of every experience and learn from every trial. As her eyes adjusted to the dark, she looked around and saw many gravestones. Compulsively trying to read them in the dim light, she learnt that these were inscribed with the names of deceased dogs. The sentiments showed that some were military dog mascots, others had died rescuing endangered people, a fair number had served politicians and royalty and most had given the ultimate sacrifice for their countries in the World

Wars. This was a graveyard to commemorate their sacrifice and honor their memory.

"It's so dark here, it gives me the creeps."

Following Kindle, all senses alert. Her heart skipped a beat, upon hearing a piercing hoot which sent a shiver down her spine. A large Great Grey Owl flew out; its wings noisily thumped the air. Confused and anxious, Raven stood still breathing heavily.

"Why did you fly at me like that?"

"You cannot see everything, I came to help you out and I can see more than you, so I can guide you through the darkness."

"Thank you, but who are you?"

"My name is Eclipse, and you are?"

"So, you're Eclipse, what a fine name, I'm Raven."

"Raven, a beautiful name for a beautiful girl."

Raven smiled upon hearing the compliment. She studied Eclipse closely, unsure whether she should allow him to join.

"Do you guys think Eclipse should join us?"

"Well, Raven, I'm guiding you, but I'd enjoy company on my flights."

"Welcome to the group, Eclipse."

"It's an honor to join."

Eclipse flew next to Kindle, and the two birds flew side by side, leading the group. Raven marveled at the fact she could understand the language of her animals.

The smell of damp soil, jasmine and rose was in the air. Raven's feet crunched on the gravelly path, snaking through the middle of the cemetery like a winding river. She listened carefully, scanning for any other signs of life or light.

She heard a loud hoot followed by screeches. A tawny owl pursued a small group of bats. The darkness was enveloping her, gripping her in its dragon like claws. But, she found the will to continue, in the bond she shared with her companions. Somehow having company took the edge off fear and unpleasantness. There was comfort in companionship.

But then a cold, sinister and menacing voice filled Raven's ears; its tone sent a cruel chill down her spine.

"You are trespassing, LEAVE!"

"Who said that?"

"Don't look now, Raven, but it appears we have bad company in the form of a zombie."

Kindle and Eclipse had spotted a creature, neither human nor animal.

"Shall we fight it off; I mean, let's hope it'll go on its way and not notice us."

Instantly, the creature vanished, but Raven was still tense for it could appear again. However, she continued to walk through the lightless graveyard, the darkness's cruel aura followed her. The dark cemetery, coupled with sudden appearance of the strange creature, made Raven frightened. The ghost of a Regimental Mascot Yorkshire Terrier named Benji appeared to her.

"Please vanquish Disquiet; he is causing terrible unease in the cemetery."

"What do you mean?"

"Look around you."

At Benji's behest, Raven surveyed the cemetery and to her surprise, she realized that the ghost dog was telling the truth. For now, the spirits of the deceased dogs were rising and snapping at one another in discord.

Raven was shocked at how the creature had caused such unrest between deceased souls formerly at peace.

"Kindle, Eclipse, both of you watch for that creature and Phantom, you and Lynk make sure you keep observant of any dangers."

"Lynk and I will keep our eyes and ears open and noses on the ground."

Raven quelled her fear by reflecting that everyone has to die someday, it's a guarantee from the moment of your birth. Some die in babyhood, childhood or youth not having lived much. Some from accidents and some later in old age having experienced and seen aplenty; different routes to the same passage. The end is the same for everyone. These thoughts stilled her mind a little, but it was hard still not to be anxious. She tried to be calm and focused.

Phantom felt Raven's fear and gently put her at ease.

"Graveyards are places of rest, remembrance, and reflection. They should be peaceful places of prayer, beauty and tranquility, where people can come and remember loved ones lost from sight but certainly still in their hearts. Their spirits move onto pastures anew, just their shells remain, just like a butterfly leaving its cocoon." Phantom explained tenderly. "Raven, you don't need to be afraid, these places commemorate and celebrate the love for those who are resting. If these dogs weren't loved or appreciated, they would have just been discarded to rot. So, you see, a cemetery is a place of love." Raven was soothed by these words and a completely different window opened in her mind.

Eclipse's eyes glowed yellow, a beam of green light shot out from them, the light identified the location of the strange creature. Adrenaline ignited Raven's spine to electrifying alertness.

"What's going on, Eclipse, what did your eyes do?"

"It's called Foresight, it helps me identify enemy locations and where they'll next appear."

"That's amazing, so do you know where that creature will appear?"

"Yes."

Hearing Eclipse's answer, Raven was empowered and alert.

"Kindle, Eclipse, do either of you see an exit anywhere?"

"Yes, Raven, it's right ahead but are you thinking of escaping or will you stay and deal with the zombie?"

Once again, the green light shot from Eclipse's eyes, the light made out a gate. However, it had also identified a shadow on the ground. Raven's instinct was to leave but there was no guarantee that anything would be better beyond the gate, because of the dark.

"What's the shadow on the ground?"

"I'm not sure but it looks to me like something might emerge from it."

"Well, if something emerges from it, let's get out of here before it does."

There in front of the gate, towering above her was the same creature that Eclipse's Foresight ability had identified; she shone the light from her scythe at it. It was a zombie with a frayed red body, two black curving horns with spikes coming out of both sides, one on either side of its reddish black head, which had two small spikes coming out of the top, narrow triangular eyes and an open yellow mouth lined with two rows of teeth. Its muscular arms that ended in claw like hands that were projecting purple light onto the graves and causing tension between the deceased.

"Who are you?"

"I am Disquiet the zombie master of fear."

"So, you're the one who told me that I would only feel fear and despair here and it's you who's causing the spirits to battle each other?"

Disquiet roared loudly; his mouth gaped as the sound came out. Raven's heart stopped for a split second. She stepped back and unsheathed her scythe and pointed the blade. Walker also drew his sword, its hilt was shaped like the wings of a flying angel, its blade long and sharp, exuding lilac laser. They stood still, observing him, watching his movements. At first, he did nothing; and kept them in suspense.

Raven noticed, the heels of Disquiet's hands had come together, and a powerful blast of dark purple energy shot from them. As the energy drew closer, Raven aimed her scythe and the amethyst lightning shot out and averted the attack.

The black sky lit up with lasers.

"Quick, we need to protect ourselves."

"Sure thing, Raven."

"Walker, you and I should deal with his long-range attacks."

Kindle and Eclipse flew at Disquiet; both speedily attacked him with their beaks and talons. Disquiet launched another blast. The blast was coming forwards, and as Raven prepared to counter, she heard a loud howl, and another blast.

"What was that?"

A stream of fiery black and purple energy in the shape of a wolf's head was shooting from Phantom's mouth. The two blasts connected, this time though, Disquiet took a hit and flinched.

"Kindle, Eclipse, I know that Disquiet has floundered, but it's only temporary, so be careful."

Raven and Walker raised their respective weapons. A brilliant white light shot from the blade of Walker's sword, while the violet thunder flowed out of Raven's scythe. The combined lasers hit Disquiet squarely, he screamed in pain from the blow.

Nevertheless, Disquiet raised his arm and swung it down; his claw like hand came down like a pitchfork. Luckily though, before it could touch any part of Raven, something bit into it. Disquiet screamed, Phantom's teeth had clamped down, digging in hard.

Disquiet lifted his arm with Phantom still hanging on. He raised it to his head, and with one mighty throw he flung Phantom off, sending him spinning across the graveyard. Raven heard a loud thud; she looked over her shoulder and saw Phantom lying against a gravestone.

"Walker, you, Lynk, Kindle and Eclipse take care of Disquiet, I'll see to Phantom."

"Raven, we'll need you to fight too."

"I can't do two things at once, Walker, right now Phantom's hurt and I have to see to him."

"Ok, Raven, do what you have to do."

Panicked, she ran towards the injured wolf, her heart thumped as she prayed that he could be saved. Upon reaching Phantom, she knelt, and with tears stinging in her eyes she gazed desperately on him.

Quickly, Raven opened the replenishing water that she stored in her cloak, while using the other hand to stroke and reassure Phantom. Pouring a few drops on the wolf's injuries.

Raven's tears flowed warm on her cheeks, and spilled off her determined chin, as she rubbed the water on his injuries, hoping it was in time to save him. Simultaneously, a horrible thought came to her, had the birds been killed?

For what seemed like a long time, she watched over Phantom anxiously. However, the wound was fully healed, and the wolf slowly began to rise. Raven smiled through her tears as Phantom rose to his feet, he licked her hand, and she affectionately stroked the back of his head.

With no time to waste, Raven was aware that Disquiet was still at large.

"Phantom, what do you say we help Walker, Lynk, Kindle and Eclipse?"

"I couldn't agree more, Raven and thank you for healing me."

Phantom followed Raven back towards the gate, where Kindle and Eclipse were aiming at Disquiet's face to stop the attack, and Walker, who was shooting light from his sword, disarming the zombie.

Disquiet, wounded, raised his arms to where Kindle and Eclipse were, and slapped the two birds away.

"As you can see, Walker, his arms are in the air, which gives us an opening, so we can hit him with a team attack."

Raven and Walker raised their weapons, bonding them together and a powerful blast of black and white energy shot out. The energy struck Disquiet hard, he shrieked in agony from the hit, but his arms returned to their normal position.

Disquiet positioned his hands together, and once again he projected a crimson and black ball. Raven deftly moved aside, though when she looked over her shoulder, Kindle looked sound asleep with his head tucked under his wing.

"What have you done?"

"I've put your nuisance bird to sleep!"

Enraged, Raven knew she had to free Kindle from his coma.

A string of black and purple circles from Disquiet's hands, hurtled towards Raven, she countered with electrical vengeance. The lightning and dark energy collided, locking together in an impasse.

Raven saw Disquiet's hand was burned black.

As soon as Disquiet's hand came towards her, Raven slashed her scythe diagonally, the blade eased through the hand and it fell to the ground. Disquiet screamed.

"Now, Raven, get rid of the stump."

"Ok, here goes."

Raven aimed her scythe at Disquiet's stump; the furious purple lightning shot out and lashed at it. A loud scream came from Disquiet; he couldn't do anything to stop the lightning.

Much to Raven's surprise and horror, a light shone on Disquiet's stump and when it faded, his hand had grown back!

"He's regenerating!"

Raven took a few steps back; her scythe was pointed at Disquiet's face. Disquiet's eyes glowed; the glow sent a freezing shiver down Raven's spine. Black energy blasts shot from them, they zoomed like jets and Raven countered with her scythe.

The purple lightning flurried out of Raven's scythe, its scorching power struck the black energy, and a thunderous explosion buffeted the whole graveyard. Dirt flew up into the air, along with small pebbles, obstructing Raven's sight, making it impossible to see Disquiet. Despite this, Raven had a brainwave; she used her scythe to hit the rocks in the zombie's direction.

When the dust cleared, Raven looked up at Disquiet, and to her surprise she noticed that there were wounds all over his body.

"It won't be long now."

"Raven, I wouldn't get excited, although he's wounded, he can still fight."

Sure enough, Eclipse was right, for Disquiet had placed his palms together, and now, a stream of black smoke was coming from his hands. Raven acted promptly, she raised her scythe and the lilac thunder rippled out of it, colliding with the lightning.

She heard Disquiet screaming in pain; a burn mark appeared on his neck. Raven watched as Disquiet clutched his neck, she stepped back, and aimed her scythe.

Disquiet removed his hand from his neck, putting it with his other hand, a black ball of energy shot from them. Magenta lightning rippled from Raven's scythe, the purple bolts and the dark energy fought. Raven's ears rang with the crash. As the smoke dissipated, Raven noticed Disquiet pitching forward.

"This is where it ends, Disquiet."

"We'll see about that."

Raven determinedly shot Disquiet with another blast. The lightning sailed forwards, Disquiet projected another blast and the two struck in an impasse.

The violet lightning prevailed as Disquiet took a hit. Then from the shadows of the night, a flock of vampire bats flew down, and carried him away. While Disquiet screamed, Raven cringed back in shock and disbelief. Kindle slowly opened his eyes and raised his head before flying back up.

"What happened to Disquiet?"

"The bats took him away before he could regenerate again."

The spirits of the dogs disappeared peacefully, and Benji's spirit approached Raven.

"Thank you for restoring peace to the sleeping souls."

"You're welcome, Benji."

Thanking Raven, Benji's spirit faded away. She hadn't noticed but the dark too had been fading away quietly. The trees now looked beautiful, no longer scary. Everything looked so serene, had she imagined all this? Had the menace of dark given rise to dark thoughts? Nevertheless a little light had vanquished the dark.

Amber's night was full of dreams, vivid dreams, her sister coming close, calling her, touching her, so real. She woke up, senses alert; breathing fast. It was only a dream! She shut her eyes tight desperate to reconnect, to continue dreaming. She needed to know what was next. If this was the only way to see and talk to her sister then she would keep her eyes closed. She tried to force sleep, to try and make the dream continue, but it felt was like she was making it happen. She needed to make the dream play out to see the message from Raven. However, she couldn't be sure what was real, what was dream, what was just imagination. She decided to keep a dream journal to interpret her dreams and wished for frequent dreams of Raven.

Dark Rise: The Nightmares' Isolation

Chapter Twenty

Music to Calm

"So much for graveyards being places of peace and rest!"

"Graveyards are peaceful and they aren't the only places in which bad things can happen. Parks and neighborhoods can be full of troublemakers, you can find fear anywhere; Raven, even in family homes." Walker responded.

She reflected on all her tests, her challenges. She couldn't really see that she was getting any closer to her goal? She seemed to be a puppet in someone else's control, what would happen if she chose not to listen to Mephistopheles, what would be her purpose, her focus. Everyone needs a focus to move forward for. Without a purpose people lose the will to live. Often being needed or useful tested a person to their very limit, but it gave one a will to get up and be useful to someone, to be needed by someone. It was strange she thought how helping someone else actually helped you back. It was a strange deception. It made one feel good. She recalled assisting the young girl in the hostel, freeing the trapped bear and Phantom, now her companion on this journey. She remembered helping Chasma to take control of her life. Each time she had gained something. Without even realizing she had gained friendship, confidence, self-esteem, wisdom, and learned problem solving. She had gained by giving!

Raven was realizing if she didn't look after her body and her mind nobody else would! Why should they? It was her job and hers alone to take care of her health, with good nutrition, fruits and vegetables, nature's gifts. She resolved to exercise; in fresh air and sunshine followed by a healing rest of mind and body.

She decided not to hurtle from one job to another–she would take care of herself and look out for her friends. Let Mephistopheles threaten all he wanted. He needed her so he would have to respect her wishes. She realized she was now less in fear of him! It had only taken a slight shift in her thinking to realize she had some control over him too. He needed her so he would have to wait!

At peace, she and her friends settled down in scenic gardens by the riverside to rest, eat and plan. She lay down looking up at the sky, relaxing and thinking, admiring the beautiful blues decorated by the whitest cloud gently moving along in the breeze, a vista so serene, peaceful, met by trees swaying to a silent rhythm.

Raven reflected that she had acquired her body at a given time and knew it would be taken away at an appointed time too, with this thought she tried to strengthen herself against fear and suspicion. After all, death was inevitable so why worry? – The body was on loan for a time to do something useful with and when time was up, it would have to be shed and returned, freeing the soul to soar to places anew.

She reflected she wanted to be a force for good, to be useful and helpful, before time was up. People feel sad when it's time to give their body back. Perhaps it was because people had not achieved all their wishes and goals and also because grieving loved ones couldn't see the soul without its body. The loss couldn't be replaced. She was brought back from these reflections by Kindle calling for her attention.

"Raven, shall we move on?"

Raven got up reluctantly, she didn't want to, but felt curious to see what was ahead.

Leaving the garden, Raven entered a new environment.She saw cultural market stalls lined up on either side. It was eerie and not a soul was at any of the stalls.

"What is this place, and why is nobody here?"

"Sorry to break up your discussion, but my Foresight has identified something in the distance."

"What?" asked Raven.

"It looks like a huge castle." Eclipse answered.

"But look what's guarding it."

"It's a gigantic serpent."

Upon hearing this, Raven shuddered, if she couldn't get past the serpent then she wouldn't be able to get into the castle or get the emerald which was hidden inside.

"I've heard tales that he's very susceptible to music."

She wondered how to deal with it; did she have to fight it?

She could hear hissing and spitting; she shivered and readied herself for what was to come. A small hummingbird flew past.

The hissing came again, turning Raven's blood to ice. Raven turned her eyes and saw a huge serpent with scales lining its body and beady eyes. The serpent was slithering right and left.

"Well, Raven, Kindle and I have found a flute stall." Eclipse told her.

"Could they be of use?" asked Raven.

"You'll just have to see for yourself and try them out, nothing ventured, nothing gained."

"Well, music can be calming, exciting, stirring, it can also be hypnotic. Have you seen how snake charmers can subdue and control snakes with a flute?"

"I would much rather pacify and relax the serpent than fight him, whilst I may win, I'd much rather try and find a non-violent solution. So, I'll try different melodies before I have to resort to fighting."

Sure enough Kindle and Eclipse were both right, for on the right-hand side was an abandoned stall, laden with countless flutes of every size, type and color. Raven glanced over the musical instruments, unsure which one was the right one, she knew that she could take no chances. Raven decided to take a plunge; she reached out, picking up a piccolo in her hand.

Raven hesitantly placed the flute to her lips; she looked around for the serpent. She didn't have long to wait before she heard the hissing and spitting from earlier, coupled with a loud slithering which grew louder as it drew closer. She could see the serpent out of the corner of her eye; it grew bigger as thundered closer towards her.

"What's the plan, Raven?"

"I think one of us will need to hold it off, while I play the flute, but whether or not the flute has any effect is another matter, who's up for holding it off?"

"I will."

"Thank you, Phantom."

In the blink of an eye, Phantom charged forwards, eyes blazing, mouth snarling and fur bristling. The serpent saw, it too charged forwards with fangs bared.

"Phantom, don't make any contact with it, remember to hold it off."

"Understood."

While Phantom and the serpent hissed and snapped at each other, Raven carried on playing the flute, the sound travelled. Much to Raven's dismay, the serpent was still hissing and lunging for Phantom. Phantom, quick on his feet, zigzagged tantalizingly in front of the serpent. The serpent slithered speedily tempted by Phantom.

"Phantom, pull back, this flute isn't having any effect; we'll have to lure him towards us."

"Are you mad, Raven?"

Reluctantly, Phantom turned back towards Raven, and began bounding forwards with the serpent not far behind, snapping and hissing. Phantom did something that amazed everyone, with his fangs glowing, he raked them down the serpent's neck, a bloody red wound appeared. The serpent hissed in pain, but the pain only succeeded in making it angrier.

"Phantom, what the hell? You've just made it angrier."

"Raven, if I hadn't injured it, it would've gone for you."

While the serpent pursued Phantom, Raven picked up an orchestral flute before following them urgently.

"Raven, what are you doing?" Walker shouted.

"Walker, I'll try a more soothing melody."

Raven repeated the same procedure, though her tune was softer than before. The soft music flowed towards the Serpent, However, instead of subduing the serpent, the beast hissed even louder, sending a sharp tremor down Raven's spine.

"Phantom, lead the serpent to the gate and detain it there, I'll bring another flute up."

Phantom continued his run, while the serpent hissed and snapped, its teeth were mere inches from his tail. Raven quickly grabbed an orchestral flute.

Raven, with the flute in hand, ran towards the gate, where she saw Phantom with the serpent pinned under his claws.

Phantom kept the serpent at bay, which was still prepared to fight, even after taking Phantom's bites. Desperately, she tried the bansuri, playing a deep melody and to her surprise, the serpent stopped hissing and coiled up, its eyes were slowly closing. The melody was taking effect; the Serpent coiled up and rested its head on its coils and drifted off.

"Phantom, come back to the group."

Phantom walked haltingly back to Raven's side, blood was flowing from his left foreleg.

"Walker, tend to Phantom"

Raven passed her healing water to Walker, before explaining what he needed to do. She had only known the wolf for a short while, but she was very attached to him.

Raven continued to play the flute to ensure the serpent was deeply asleep.

"Walker, how's Phantom?"

"His leg's no longer bleeding, and he can put weight on it."

"That's good, thanks, Walker.

As the serpent slept, the castle gates swung open. It was just a matter of walking through.

Dark Rise: The Nightmares' Isolation

Chapter Twenty-One

Chasm of Challenges

Expansive gardens surrounded the imposing castle. Demon heads stood atop each column and pillar. Their stony evil eyes and sneering grin made Raven roll her eyes and snigger at poor taste, clearly designed to spread fear and superstition. In the past this would have scared Raven. She was no longer frightened by these vulgar and cowardly displays.

As Raven and Walker strode vigilantly towards the castle, a bright green glow exuded from Raven's silver ring. Excited by seeing this glow, she realized with a thrill, that she was near one of the gems that Mephistopheles had put her through all these ordeals for! When Mephistopheles had given her the ring- he had told her that as she got close to the stone the ring would glow. Now, at long last it really was glowing! Delighted with this knowledge, she felt a mixture of curiosity and excitement.

"I think there's a stone in the castle; I just hope we can get it easily and amicably!" said Raven.

"There's something surrounding the castle."

"It's a force field to defend it." Walker replied.

"We need to think of a plan to get through it."

Brainstorming ideas on how to get past the barrier, they decided to use their individual abilities in unison.

"We need to find out what's generating the barrier."

Kindle and Eclipse circled the castle, looking around for the source of the barrier.

"Raven, we've spotted pale green power crystals projecting the barrier from beneath the rocks in the small surrounding stream."

"Great!"

"Let's disable the power crystals and then it'll disappear, in fact, you and Lynk take one side and Phantom, and I will take the other."

"Kindle, you and Eclipse will need to scout for any dangers"

Raven pointed her scythe at the power crystal to the southeast corner, dark purple lightning streamed towards it, while Phantom fired a fiery wolf-shaped energy blast from his mouth. The united forces struck the power crystal, destroying it and removing one section of the electrical field.

"Walker, how's it going?"

"I've knocked out a power crystal as well!"

"Fantastic."

"Phantom, let's take out the other crystal on this side."

The coast was still clear, so Raven and Phantom shot towards the other crystal, and struck the force field, while Walker and Lynk poised themselves on the other side. There was a crescendo of lightning as the force field fizzled out.

Kindle and Eclipse flew above Raven, as they entered the castle's vast and grand great hall. Raven surveyed the great hall from its stained-glass floor to its walls adorned with pictures of a black-skinned satyr creature with glowing red eyes. The green glow that exuded from her ring grew more vibrant in its brilliance. It was leading and guiding her. Her ears pricked up when she heard a loud shaking sound.

"The ground is shaking." Raven snapped.

The shaking split the great hall into three platforms above her. Confused, Raven looked over the platforms, unsure of what was ahead.

Raven jumped and grabbed the rigid edge of the first floor and pulled herself up. The others joined her, trying to figure out the challenge. Her ring's glow illuminated as she looked in front of her and saw a blank slate with several puzzle pieces next to it.

"It looks like you have to do the puzzle for as long as the egg timer allows."

Quick as lightning, she put the four corner pieces in, whilst glancing at the egg timer, carefully putting the bottom row into place, before doing the right side.

Raven's eyes were darting to the sand timer, watching as the black sand trickled down. With a confident grin, she put the middle pieces in, completing it before the sand reached the bottom. Raven flung her arms up in a victory pose, eyes shining with a big grin on her face.

"Good job, Raven."

"This is the sort of challenge I like."

Feeling confident and elated, she was keen to follow the flashing and brightening light of the ring across to the next platform, with Phantom and the birds. Summoning the courage to jump, she reached the higher platform. She was slipping off. Walker gently pulled her up, and not for the first time Raven found herself grateful for her helpful friends.

She saw five magicians, each holding two sticks, one in either hand. Another stick lay in the basket on Raven's right side, and the green glow on her ring was irradiating brighter. Reading the ring, she instinctively picked the stick up in her right hand. She observed the magicians to ensure that she would know what move to make.

"Shall we throw first, or will you?"

"What were the magicians talking about? Why would they want to throw their sticks?"

"You throw first." Said Raven nervously.

The magicians threw down their sticks and to Raven's horror, rattlesnakes with small, beady eyes and forked tongues were now writhing in front of her. The tips of their tails rattled, as they hissed menacingly at her. Standing frozen, uncertainly staring at the rattlesnakes, her fear of snakes rising. Her eyes were wide with dread, mesmerized by the magicians' magic. She shook as she saw the snakes slithering towards her.

In her distress, Raven petitioned her deity for inspiration, her silent secret power in times of stress. Answers came, as her mind received inspiration from her silent support.

"Tell me what I must do."

"*Raven, you must throw down what is in your right hand, their snakes are mere illusions faked with magic, you must trust, yours will devour their magic.*"

Fear is your imagination. The realities are not as scary, try and see.

Inspired, she swept her staff towards the snakes, they slid back, so she advanced and swept it again. She was shocked to find her staff slithered out of her hand; she had been wielding a snake! It was a large black forest cobra with a yellow underbelly and a terrifying look! The cobra hissed and flicked its forked tongue at the rattlesnakes; the rattlesnakes hissed back.

In an electrified movement, the cobra devoured the rattlesnakes. They were all gone! The magicians watched in disbelief and horror their defeat.

Raven picked up the cobra which had become a staff again. Her strong trust in a universal creator had helped her override her phobia of snakes, one of her worst fears. Empowered, she confidently flung herself onto the next level. On doing so, the glow on Raven's ring brightened much more.

As the others joined her, Raven saw several Hobgoblins, all of them wearing futuristic armor, some on foot, clasping scimitars, whilst others rode huge salamanders, whilst gripping sharp, lethal spears.

"Charge and destroy them!" the hobgoblin war boss shrieked as he led the hobgoblins to attack.

"Remember, everyone, although we're outnumbered, we can beat them if we work together." said Raven.

The hobgoblins charged forwards; the cold steel blades of their scimitars gleamed ominously. Raven readied her scythe, gripping its hilt tightly as she prepared for the advancing hobgoblin foot soldiers. Meanwhile, Walker who was once again armored, had readied his sword to defend, as Phantom, Lynk and the birds prepared to fight the cavalry.

Without second thoughts she swung her scythe and its blade ate through three hobgoblins, they screamed as they fell off the platform. While Raven knocked another hobgoblin off, she saw a striking white light burn the armor on one more, before the light scorched its skin.

She glanced over her shoulder, seeing Phantom head-butting a hobgoblin and its salamander off of the edge. Raven's heart skipped a beat, for when she looked down, the hobgoblin lay spread eagled with something protruding through its body.

Momentarily distracted by the dead hobgoblin below, Raven let her guard down. At the same time, a bloody gash appeared on her left arm; she looked at her wound and saw a hobgoblin, its scimitar, wet with blood, her blood. Quick as lightning, Raven took a sip of her healing water and her wound healed.

She stood up, scythe in hand, and with one mighty swing she knocked the last hobgoblins over the edge.

The hobgoblins defeated, Raven raced onto the bridge ahead, rushing towards the huge door beyond. Looking back, she noticed cracks quickly forming on the poorly cemented bridge, creeping up on her!

Panicked, she quickened her footsteps as the bridge began falling apart. She hoped anxiously that Phantom would get across.

Suddenly, a black blur leapt past the bridge, she recognized Phantom! Bits of the bridge were now falling.

Just as she reached the end, the last part of the bridge crumbled, and she plummeted with it. Faced with certain death on the spikes below, Raven desperately looked around for something to grab onto. However, as she fell, a pair of hands grabbed her round the shoulders, and carried her back up to the platform.

Turning to face her rescuer, she saw the familiar angel wings of Walker, and at that she smiled broadly.

"Walker, you saved my life, thank you!"

"We're a team, Raven; we look out for one another." Walker said gently.

Now on the final platform, Raven noticed the glow of her ring was much, much brighter than before. This was good, a sign that she was close to the gem. A tall stone archway stood at the end, and floating just in front of it was the emerald! Amazed and elated, Raven reached out to take it. Raven thought the emerald would be extremely difficult to attain, but she reached for it and to her great surprise and wonderment it willingly moved towards her! Amazement and happiness washed over Raven as she watched it draw closer to her hand, she couldn't believe her eyes, it was as if the emerald trusted her to protect and safeguard it.

John Rahway

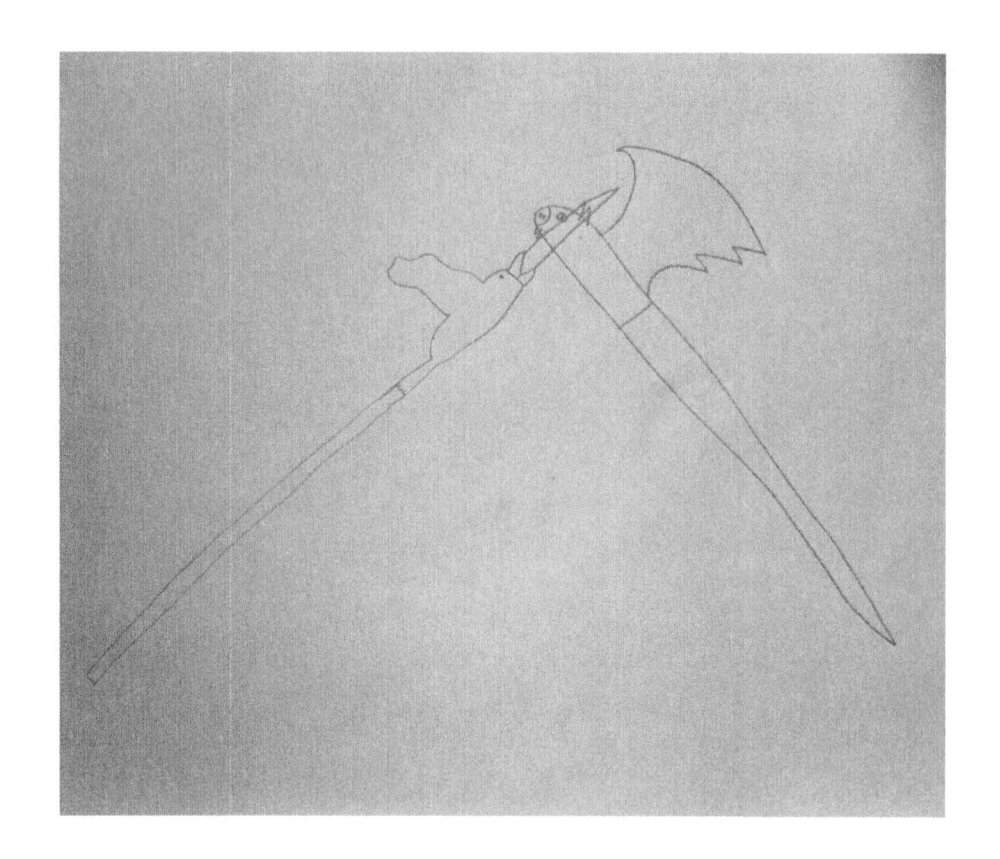

Chapter Twenty-Two
Price of Victory

Raven followed Kindle and Eclipse through the huge arch, into a throne room, and saw the same portrait from the entrance hall, hung high above the seat. Seated on the throne, with a scepter in his right hand, was the satyr like creature from the portrait! Raven froze in shock and disbelief. Could this be the one who ruled The Nightmare Rift or even worse one of Mephistopheles's servants?

"Who are you?" She questioned.

"Welcome, Raven, I am Phobetor Greek God of Nightmares, the first of Mephistopheles's trusted aides, ruler of The Nightmare Rift. I congratulate you for making it thus far. I applaud your courage." Phobetor saluted with a smile that showed his hideous teeth, an insincere smile that didn't reach his cold yellow eyes. "Mightier people than you have attempted to claim the emerald, but none have succeeded." He boomed. "I have power enough to get it, but it doesn't yield to me or my soldiers. It is surrounded by a magical barrier that is impenetrable by might and power. I can't imagine that a mere girl like you can attain it with your scrawny group of friends." He laughed mockingly. "I'll be generous and allow you to leave in safety. I can't believe Mephistopheles chose a little girl for such an important task."

Raven couldn't believe her ears; she already had the emerald in the deep pocket of her cloak. But she said, "Thank you, sire, I'm grateful." She was desperate to leave before he realized. She turned tail and walked briskly, eyes wide.

"STOP!"

Raven's heart stopped momentarily, fight or flight took over and she bolted. But he was upon her.

Phobetor looked on open mouthed, furious, and shocked!

"How did this young damsel come and just pick up the emerald just like that! Without a struggle, without a sound! How is that even possible?"

Raven stared him down confidently. She knew that he would do everything he could to prevent her from keeping the emerald. She wouldn't let him have it; she had worked too hard and had been through too many challenging trials for it. She simply couldn't afford to let her hard work go to waste by allowing it to fall into evil hands. Especially not Mephistopheles's.

"Hand me the emerald now."

"I will not surrender it to you or Mephistopheles."

"Very well then. I have no choice but to kill you. To ensure none of your strange friends interfere, they're tied up."

She looked around. Raven saw Walker, Phantom and Lynk tied up in ropes. Angered and dismayed, she readied herself to fight not just for herself but for her friends also.

Raven and Phobetor paced round each other, weapons in hand, summing up the enemy. Phobetor pointed his scepter ruthlessly. A stream of energy flowed from the three prongs. With the quickness of a panther, Raven defended. The lightning shot from her scythe, blocking the dark energy.

Raven slashed her scythe, its blade coming down fast, slamming Phobetor's scepter. A deafening clang rang out, as the metal of the two weapons met. Sparks flew. She pushed back with all her might.

Phobetor grunted as he fell. Raven quickly took advantage, and once again, the bright purple thunder shot from the scythe, as she electrocuted him. Phobetor roared, rose up, seized his scepter and attacked.

The black energy cascaded forwards. Raven struck back. An explosion flooded the throne room. The smoke cleared to reveal Phobetor wounded on the ground, black blood flowing from his chest. Raven glanced towards her friends, the birds had freed Phantom, Lynk and Walker had slid out of the ropes using angel powers.

Seeing Phobetor wounded, she moved purposefully, raised her scythe, to bring it down on his neck. Just as the blade was in position, she saw Phobetor, fully healed, jump up.

"The red healing mineral vapors in the corners of the room." Phobetor gloated, seeing her shocked expression.

Realizing that Phobetor was using the red mineral vapor energy to heal himself, she knew she was fighting a losing battle until she could destroy the source.

"That's it, Phobetor, you're going down."

"Such bravado for a scared little girl."

Raven and Phobetor pushed with all their might, each determined to overpower the other. Phobetor advanced, poised to finish Raven off.

Raven kicked out, her shoes slammed into his stomach. Phobetor pitched backwards, falling heavily, while Raven kicked back to a vertical base and swung her scythe strategically.

Phobetor retaliated. The two weapons clanged. She reaimed her scythe; the electricity tore from the blade, zapping Phobetor to the floor.

As the Greek Nightmare God rose, Raven boldly thrust her right knee into his stomach, before striking him down.

"Some god!"

Phobetor pointed his scepter at the red vapor. The red energy flowed through his sceptre, into his body, healing his wounds, restoring him to health and vigor.

"No matter how many times you wear me down, I'll always be able to heal."

Raven realized she had to make the healing vapors inaccessible to Phobetor.

"Walker, Lynk, can you deactivate the vapors. He's using them to regenerate."

Raven activated her scythe, thunder clapped out, striking Phobetor, knocking him to the floor. Her enemy grounded, Raven plunged the blade into his back. Phobetor seemed unaffected, dragged himself to his feet, picking up his sceptre, striking Raven in the stomach. The blow knocked Raven back; she held her stomach in pain. But then, she saw Walker and Lynk destroying the vapors. This encouraged her to face Phobetor.

Instead she saw a circle of Phobetors surrounding her, holding their scepters. Raven's blood froze; she looked fretfully around her, trying to discern the real enemy. Phobetor was enjoying Raven's confusion; it made him feel clever and invincible. Gloating with self-importance. He started to smell victory. His smug smirk said it all. He thought to himself, she would see so many opponents, would be overwhelmed and concede defeat. He had forgotten her strange friends. He waved his scepter in circular motion, and he projected a small cyclone.

"Which one's real?"

"Raven, my Foresight has identified that to find the real one; you have to stop the wind that's blowing round you."

Raven dragged her scythe in a circle, pushing the fierce wind back with the lightning from her scythe. The holograms disappeared, leaving the real Phobetor standing alone, looking pathetic. Emboldened Raven took one mighty swing at the target. The bolt hit home, knocking him to the floor with a crash. Phobetor fervently looked for the healing vapors.

"It's finished, Phobetor! Consider this the end of the line for you!"

Phobetor was lying on the ground, barely alive, mortally wounded. Raven was standing, exhausted, but standing, she dragged herself forwards and finished him.

Exhausted, she turned her attention to the case holding the scrolls; the purple lightning shot out of her scythe, shattering the glass case, reducing the scrolls to mere ash. Finally, one of Mephistopheles's relics containing part of his soul was destroyed! He had taken the precaution to separate his soul into six pieces, thus rendering himself immortal. Raven had just destroyed the first piece of his soul.

A hologram of Mephistopheles appeared screaming in pain.

"What is this defiance? It seems to me that you do not have any interest in regaining your memory."

"Look, Mephistopheles, you can't tell me what to do."

"The ramifications of your treachery will be severe."

Mephistopheles melted away, leaving her feeling scared.

"You did it, Raven."

"Phobetor's defeated now, let's leave."

Walker led them through a portal. Raven found herself in a street, just like the one where her journey had begun. However, a warm healing breeze lifted her spirits a little, as she tried to process Mephistopheles's threats and tried to forget them.

"Go to the house at the end of the road."

"Who said that?"

"It is I Dali swallow of wind."

Raven saw a beautiful swallow flying beside her.

"Walker, this swallow, just told me to go to the house at the end."

"She's directing us towards somewhere to live."

"It might be a trap."

"Not everything is a trap, Raven."

"I must defeat Mephistopheles, hopefully I'll find a way to do that, and I can't relax my guard until he's powerless. I won't let him get his hands on the precious gems. They represent kindness, compassion, love, diligence, trust and humility and Mephistopheles would use them to destroy all that's good and create disharmony for power and control."

Raven kept her thoughts in her head, as she couldn't risk Mephistopheles knowing her plans.

She saw the house!

She picked up the key under the doormat, placed it in the door and immediately felt peace and safety, the house was cozy and felt safe. She walked around, explored a little, opened a wardrobe and saw clothes, her size. She hung her cloak.

Raven sat comfortably on the bed, reflecting on how to defeat Mephistopheles. She noticed a demonic looking greatsword with a serrated blade which exuded a red glow, with a note next to it. She examined the greatsword and read the note:

Raven

Mom told me to give you Soulshadow before she left, use it well

Your loving sister Amber.

Raven sat down, wondering who Amber could be, and whose mother was indicated in the letter. Could it be her mother? Could it be that she was getting closer to her family? Raven didn't dare to dream in case she was to be disappointed.

John Rahway

Dark Rise: The Nightmares' Isolation

John Rahway

Epilogue

Phobetor was defeated, Raven had left his broken body unattended on the floor of his throne room. His body became prey to a sorceress. Viessa was aware of her power and strength she walked in arrogantly, stopping momentarily to admire her reflection in the mirror. Footsteps confident and light, she knelt beside the dead body. With strong hands, she cut and ripped the still-warm heart from Phobetor's carcass. Feeling proud of her bravery and strength, she was aglow with self-appreciation.

All too soon, Viessa realized she wasn't alone, for Mephistopheles appeared before her. She presented the heart in a show of loyalty and respect for her master.

"Eat the heart, eat it" he hissed.

Viessa fought to hide her distaste and smothered her grimace.

"The deal was to present you the heart."

He said again "Eat the heart, eat it."

Deflated with her short-lived victory, she turned away from him to hide her anger and disgust as her pride took a nosedive.

"Is there another way to reanimate the dead?" stalled Viessa.

"The heart will give you the powers to reanimate the dead."

Her strength was replaced by disgust as she consumed Phobetor's heart. A bright green glow exuded from her dark blue eyes and then her body, for she had gained the ability to reanimate the deceased. A rare talent indeed!

The thought crossed her mind about the possible consequences of resurrecting the dead, but she wanted the power.

Phobetor's death meant that the Dead Sea scroll containing one of the six pieces of Mephistopheles' soul had been destroyed. Mephistopheles was weakened. The other pieces of his soul were guarded by Nergal the Mesopotamian god of plagues, Orochi the Japanese eight headed dragon god and Anubis the Egyptian god of death. She didn't know Chernobog was going to be resurrected to guard a piece of his soul.

"Well, Viessa, you can now raise the dead, so go to The Elemental Sanctum, and resurrect Chernobog, so he can guard the relic that holds another piece of my soul." Mephistopheles ordered.

"As you command, my lord." Viessa was eager to try out her new power! "Mephistopheles, where must I go?"

"Go to the River of Sorrow under the Weeping Waterfall in The Elemental Sanctum."

After giving Viessa her directive, Mephistopheles disappeared, and the sorceress entered a portal. She stepped through, leaving The Nightmare Rift behind.

Viessa moved purposefully forwards like a stalking cheetah, excited to try out her new power.

"I will gain Mephistopheles' favour." she knew he was master of the dark arts and powerful. She was ambitious, very ambitious. The dark arts enthralled her.

Before long, Viessa was at the bank of the River of Sorrow, its dark purple water churned like tears of pain. A small boat was docked at the riverbank, and Viessa boarded it.

As she rowed, the river churned and splashed aggressively. Suddenly, several crying water nymphs guarding the river appeared and made wailing noises. She cautiously extracted her staff which bore a sharp glass crystal at the top, which illuminated the darkness. She was ready to strike any who dared challenge her.

The crying nymphs annoyed the sorceress. Viessa ruthlessly disposed of them with the power of her staff, calmly dipping the staff in the river, cleansing it of their blood.

Viessa rowed to the waterfall and found a bright orange energy shield. She raised her staff; dark blue lightning flowed from the now glowing glass crystal, striking the shield, until it cracked. Fragments of the orange light flew away, the force field fell to the ground like shattered glass.

Holding the skirt of her floor length black dress, Viessa exited the boat, stepping onto the dark threshold. Moss and thorny trees lined either side of the body of water. The beautiful amethyst and the reliquary crown of the Roman Emperor were placed atop two pillars. A large statue of Chernobog stood in the center. With her new power, Viessa held out her staff and Phobetor's life force flowed through the crystal, into the statue.
Swarms of vampire bats took flight round the dark waterfall, engulfing the cave in the blackest shadow.

The life force crackled into the statue like a new soul. Chernobog's eyes glowed orange while the stone disintegrated. Viessa pointed her staff skywards and fired bright green lighting. The grey-black skies of The Elemental Sanctum opened. A deluge of acid rain fell from the full clouds, speeding up the resurrection.

The rock melted from Chernobog's body and revealed him part by part. The bats flew round, screeching with delight.

The rock surrounding Chernobog's head flaked and fell off. The newly resurrected Chernobog let out a roar that shook The Elemental Sanctum.

"Ah, this body feels so right, I feel strong and powerful, but who are you, sorceress?"

"Chernobog, that's no way to speak to the one who has resurrected you."

As Viessa turned to leave, Mephistopheles appeared, and the nefarious god bowed while the sorceress curtseyed before him.

"Well done, Viessa."

"Your praise honours me, Mephistopheles."

"Now, Viessa, you must go to Darkholme Castle and aid the Coalition of Darkness."

"Yes, my lord."

"Chernobog, Phobetor is dead, and Raven has the emerald, and she has destroyed the first of my relics and my immortality depends on the existence of the relics."

"What is my reward for retrieving the emerald from Raven?" asked Chernobog.

"You will be my second in command." Mephistopheles answered.

"He's getting such an easy job, but I've resurrected him." Viessa thought bitterly.

Mephistopheles was unfinished; he turned to Chernobog with pleasure in his eyes. Engrossed in planning with Chernobog, he had overlooked that Viessa was still listening, eavesdropping, and covertly watching. Chernobog's desire to be Mephistopheles' second in command filled him with twisted loyalty. Satisfied, Mephistopheles teleported to his throne in Inferno.

Viessa looked at Chernobog; a sting of bitterness hit her because she had gone to the trouble of resurrecting him. Now she felt overlooked, discarded, rejected, and excluded.

Printed in Great Britain
by Amazon